呦呦鹿鸣

美得窒息的诗经

许渊冲 译　闫红 解析

汉英对照

长江出版传媒

长江文艺出版社

目录

Contents

君子 × 偕老

第 一 章

CHAPTER ONE

She'd live with her lord till old

周南·兔罝

肃肃兔罝（jū），椓之丁丁。赳赳武夫，公侯干城。

肃肃兔罝，施于中逵。赳赳武夫，公侯好仇。

肃肃兔罝，施于中林。赳赳武夫，公侯腹心。

The Rabbit Catcher

Well set are rabbit nets;
On the pegs go the blows.
The warrior our lord gets
 Protects him from the foes.

Well set are rabbit nets,
Placed where crossroads appear.
The warrior our lord gets
Will be his good compeer.

Well set are rabbit nets,
Amid the forest spread.
The warrior our lord gets
Serves him with heart and head.

君子偕老

捕猎的兔网被密密拉起，结实的木桩被叮叮当当地敲击。你看那雄赳赳的武夫，为公侯筑就坚固城池。

捕猎的兔网被密密拉起，就设在那看似四通八达的路口。你看那雄赳赳的武夫，是公侯的好帮手。

捕猎的兔网被密密拉起，半隐半现于密林之中。你看那雄赳赳的武夫，是公侯们的心腹。

张爱玲曾说古人有一种共同的宇宙观："文官执笔安天下，武将上马定乾坤。"在动辄是战争离乱的年代，看到那些军备与战士，就会让人产生安全感。当然这未免天真，但草芥般的百姓，也只能以这样一厢情愿的信任保持内心的稳定。

召南·甘棠

蔽芾甘棠，勿翦勿伐，召伯所茇。

蔽芾甘棠，勿翦勿败，召伯所憩。

蔽芾甘棠，勿翦勿拜，召伯所说。

The Duke of Shao

O leafy tree of pear!
Don't clip or make it bare,
For once our Duke lodged there.
O leafy tree of pear!
Don't break its branches bare,
For once our Duke rested there.
O leafy tree of pear!
Don't bend its branches bare,
For once our Duke halted there.

若你经过那棵茂盛的棠梨树，
请一定要善待它，
别剪它的枝叶，别折断它的条干，
因为召伯曾在此处居住。

若你经过那棵茂盛的棠梨树，
请一定要善待它，
别剪它的枝叶，别折断它的条干，
因为召伯曾经倚着它休憩。

若你经过那棵茂盛的棠梨树，
请一定要善待它，
别剪它的枝叶，别折断它的条干，
因为召伯曾在此处停歇。

　　我们常常是因为爱一些人，而更加爱这
个世界的。他们步履所及，目之所见，皆成
其为好。召伯即召公奭，曾经帮周武王灭商。
传说他曾在甘棠树下会见民众，听讼断狱。

①芟：草舍也，居住。②说：通"税"，休息。

召南·驺虞

彼茁者葭，壹发五豝bā，于嗟乎驺虞！

彼茁者蓬，壹发五豵zōng，于嗟乎驺虞！

A Hunter

Abundant rushes grow along;
One arrow hits one boar among.
Ah! What a hunter strong!

Abundant reeds along the shores!
One arrow scares five boars.
Ah! What a hunter one adores!

一

君子偕老

　　隔着茁壮的芦苇丛，看那猎手多么英武，一下子射中五只母猪，天哪，这猎人多么英武！

　　隔着那茁壮的飞蓬，看那猎手多么英武，一下子射中五只小猪，天哪，这猎人多么英武！

　　不管是围猎还是观看围猎，都能够刺激到肾上腺素的分泌，何况还是在春天！这首诗一再咏叹，飞扬之感尽在眼前。

邶风·旄丘

旄丘之葛兮，何诞之节兮。叔兮伯兮，何多日也？

何其处也？必有与也！何其久也？必有以也！

狐裘蒙戎，匪车不东。叔兮伯兮，靡所与同。

瑣兮尾兮，流离之子。叔兮伯兮，褎如充耳。

Refugees

The high mound's vines appear
So long and wide.
O uncles dear,
Why not come to our side?

Why dwell you thereamong
For other friends you make?
Why stay so long?
For who else' sake?

Furs in a mess appear;
Eastward goes not your cart.
O uncles dear,
Don't you feel sad at heart?

So poor and base appear
We refugees.
O uncles dear,
Why don't you listen, please?

一 君子偕老

山坡上的葛藤，枝蔓已经拖得老长。

卫国的兄弟啊，时日渐久，为什么让我等到心中恓惶。

为什么你们能若无其事地安生度日？也许自有你们的缘故？

为什么忘记允诺一味迁延？可能有更好的盘算。

逃亡时穿的狐皮袍子，已经敝旧如飞蓬，你们的车队从不曾向东。

我的兄弟们啊，我们的处境多么不同。

卑微如我，流离失所。

我的兄弟们啊，你们却只是微笑着走过，对我的悲伤充耳不闻。

公元前 594 年，狄人迫逐黎侯，黎侯流亡到卫，指望卫伯主持公道，后来发现只是一厢情愿。这首诗写出从期待到绝望的全过程。小人物的人间清醒，只是让自己更受伤，黎侯的心情普通人也能体会。

①狐裘蒙戎：狐裘皮毛凌乱。

邶风·北门

出自北门，忧心殷殷。终窭且贫，莫知我艰。
已焉哉！天实为之，谓之何哉！

王事适我，政事一埤益我。我入自外，室人
交遍谪我。已焉哉！天实为之，谓之何哉！

王事敦我，政事一埤遗我。我入自外，室人
交遍摧我。已焉哉！天实为之，谓之何哉！

A Petty Official

Out of north gate
Sadly I go.
I'm poor by fate.
Who knows my woe?
Let it be so!
Heaven wills this way.
What can I say?

I am busy about
Affairs of royalty.
When I come from without,
I'm blamed by family.

So let it be!
Heaven wills this way.
What can I say?

I am busier about
Public affairs, but oh!
When I come from without,
I'm given blow on blow.
Let it be so!
Heaven wills this way.
What can I say?

我默默走出北门，带着一脑门官司。

像我这样又窘迫又穷困，谁能懂我的艰辛。

算了吧，这就是我的命，老天如此安排，再说又有何用？

上面的事儿派给我，公事一股脑地叫我做。

疲惫不堪回到家，家里人轮番指责我。

算了吧，这就是我的命，再说又有何用？

上面的事儿派给我，政务全部叫我做。

想回家找点安慰，家里人也轮番指责我。

算了吧，这就是我的命，再说又有何用？

　　一个失意小吏的碎碎念。钱少活多压力大，到家还被家里人百般挑剔，很像张爱玲小说里的场景，疲惫茫然的中年男人，在自身与他人那里都找不到认同。他一次次说着算了吧，但还是一次次念叨着，心中有无限的委屈与不甘。从他身上，可以看到现代职场加班人的影子。

鄘风·墙有茨

墙有茨，不可埽也。中冓_{gòu}之言，不可道也。
所可道也，言之丑也。

墙有茨，不可襄也。中冓之言，不可详也。
所可详也，言之长也。

墙有茨，不可束也。中冓之言，不可读也。
所可读也，言之辱也。

Scandals

The creepers on the wall
Cannot be swept away.
Stories of inner hall
Should not be told by day.
What would have to be told
Is scandals manifold.

The creepers on the wall
 Cannot be rooted out.
Scandals of inner hall
Should not be talked about.
If they are talked of long,
They'll be an endless song.

The creepers on the wall
Cannot be together bound.
Scandals of inner hall
Should not be spread around.
If spread from place to place,
They are shame and disgrace.

一 君子偕老

墙上有蒺藜草，不能把它扫。
宫中的那些话，不足为外人道。
要是跟人说，实在不光彩。

墙上有蒺藜草，不能将它除。
宫中的那些话，不要细说它。
要是细说它，那可就太长啦。

墙上有蒺藜草，不能捆成束。
宫中的那些话，不能到处讲。
要是到处讲，脸面何处藏。

　　卫国公子顽与庶母私通，这八卦传入民间，娱乐了大众。但这首诗显然更胜一筹，像《红楼梦》里薛宝钗所言，"将市俗的粗话，撮其要，删其繁，再加润色比方出来，一句是一句"。点到为止，欲说还休，妙在彼此心领神会。在无法直接对抗时，幽默是刺穿荒诞最有力的武器。

鄘风·君子偕老

君子偕老，副笄六珈。委委佗佗，如山如河，象服是宜。子之不淑，云如之何？

玼兮玼兮，其之翟也。鬒发如云，不屑髢也；玉之瑱也，象之揥也，扬且之皙也。胡然而天也？胡然而帝也？

① 瑳兮瑳兮，其之展也。蒙彼绉绤，是绁袢也。② ③

子之清扬，扬且之颜也。展如之人兮，邦之媛也！

Duchess Xuan Jiang of Wei

She'd live with her lord till old,
Adorned with gems and gold.
Stately and full of grace,
Stream-like, she went her pace.
As a mountain she'd dwell;
Her robe became her well.
Raped by the father of her lord,
O how could she not have been bored!

She is so bright and fair
In pheasant-figured gown.
Like cloud is her black hair,
No false locks but her own.

Her earrings are of jade,
Her pin ivory-made.
Her forehead's white and high,
Like goddess from the sky.

She is so fair and bright
In rich attire snow-white.
O'er her fine undershirt
She wears close-fitting skirt.
Her eyes are bright and clear;
Her face will facinate.
Alas! Fair as she might appear,
She's a raped beauty of the state.

一 君子偕老

你是那与君子偕老的人，珠环翠绕玉搔头。
你仪态舒缓，如山如河，华丽的礼服与你正相宜。
然而你德不配位，让人怎么说？

绚烂如霞是你绣着山鸡的礼服。
你黑发浓密，不屑垫入假发掩饰苍老。
美玉耳环，垂在你鬓边叮当。
象牙做的簪子，插在你的鬓边。
你广颐方额肌肤胜雪，多么像天仙，又多么像
帝女。

鲜艳璀璨，是展示你身份的礼服。
精细的葛布，做成你夏日的内衣。
你眼神明亮，眉宇宽广。
你这样的一个人啊，真是国中的大美人。

　　这首诗据说是讽刺卫宣公的妻子宣姜。
卫宣公原本为儿子伋聘娶宣姜，见她貌美，
据为己有。后来，宣姜又被迫嫁给伋的弟弟公
子顽。

　　宣姜的一生身不由己，但在当时被视为
红颜祸水。不过对于声名狼藉的女人，公众的
态度是批判里带着好奇。这首诗宣布宣姜道
德破产的同时，对她的衣饰和容貌一再描摹，
雍容华贵的主体色调下还有一丝诱惑，是大
众对于身份高贵的绯闻女主角的想象。

①瑳：朱熹译为鲜盛貌。②展：礼服。③绉绤：夏天所穿白色内衣。

鄘风·定之方中

定之方中，作于楚宫。揆之以日，作于楚室。

树之榛栗，椅桐梓漆，爰伐琴瑟。

升彼虚矣，以望楚矣。望楚与堂，景山与京。

降观于桑，卜云其吉，终焉允臧。

灵雨既零，命彼倌人。星言夙驾，说于桑田。

匪直也人，秉心塞渊。騋牝三千。

lái
pìn

Duke Wen of Wei

At dusk the four stars form a square;
 It's time to build a palace new.
The sun and shade determine where
To build the Palace at Chu,
To plant hazel and chestnut trees,
Fir, yew, plane, cypress. When cut down,
They may be used to make lutes to please
The ducal crown.

The duke ascends the ruined wall
To view the site of capital
And where to build his palace hall.

He then surveys the mountain's height
And comes down to see mulberries.
The fortune-teller says it's right
And the duke is pleased with all these.

After the fall of vernal rain
The duke orders his groom to drive
His horse and cab with might and main.
At mulberry fields they arrive;
To farmers he is good indeed
He wishes husbandry to thrive
And three thousand horses to breed.

定星照在正中，这是十月，他在楚丘建造宫殿。

他查看日影，建造宫室。

栽种树木，比如榛，比如栗，比如椅，比如桐，比如梓，比如漆，待它们长大，伐做琴瑟，祭祀先祖。

他登上漕邑故墟，看楚丘全貌。

看那高地与城邑，走遍大山与高陵。

他走下来，观察桑园，虔诚地占卜，得到佳音，知晓是应许之地。

好雨在窗外零落，他叫上他的马夫。

待到雨落星出就出门，停在桑园。

他所做的还不只这些，用心实在又深沉。

他的付出没有白费，已经拥有三千七尺骏马。

狄人攻破卫国，卫戴公率领残部暂居漕邑。之后卫文公继位，他励精图治，在楚丘营造宫室。这首诗讲述的就是卫文公文治武功的过程。

卫文公勤勉又踏实，上问天意，下察民情，中兴基业，将心中的蓝图一步步实现。

鄘风·载驰

载驰载驱，归唁卫侯。驱马悠悠，言至于漕。

大夫跋涉，我心则忧。

既不我嘉，不能旋反。视尔不臧，我思不远。

既不我嘉，不能旋济？视尔不臧，我思不閟。

陟彼阿丘，言采其蝱。女子善怀，亦各有行。

许人尤之，众稚且狂。 zhì

我行其野，芃芃其麦。控于大邦，谁因谁极？

大夫君子，无我有尤。百尔所思，不如我所之。

I climb the sloping mound
To pick toad-lilies round.
Of woman don't make light!
My heart knows what is right.
My countrymen put blame
On me and feel no shame.

I go across the plains;
Thick and green grow the grains.
I'll plead to mighty land,
Who'd hold out helping hand.
"Deputies, don't you see
The fault lies not with me?
Whatever may think you,
It's not so good as my view."

I gallop while I go
To share my brother's woe.
I ride down a long road
To my brother's abode.
The deputies will thwart
My plan and fret my heart.

"Although you say me nay,
I won't go back the other way.
Conservative are you
While farsight'd is my view?"
"Although you say me nay,
I won't stop on my way.
Conservative are you,
I can't accept your view."

君子偕老

一

策马奔腾，我去慰问失国的卫侯。

快马加鞭，我跨越迢迢路途，遥见漕城的轮廓。

回头却见许国大夫跋涉而来，要将我阻拦令我忧伤。

你们反对我继续前行，我也不能立即跟你们踏上征程。

看你们也没好主意，我不能做太远的指望。

你们反对我继续前行，我也不能转身再次渡过那河流。

看你们也没有好主意，我的思虑不能到此打住。

登上山丘，采摘贝母。

女子虽然经常多愁善感，但也能付诸行动。

许国人只会抱怨，我看你们幼稚又张狂。

我走在田野上，麦苗茂盛，欣欣向荣。

你们快去向大国求救，看看有谁能援助。

只说不做的大夫君子们啊，不要只会抱怨我。

你们寻思千百遍，不如我亲自去看一看。

　　卫国被狄人攻破后，卫懿公之女，已经嫁到许国的许穆夫人要去慰问卫侯，被许国大夫阻止。他们指责她感情用事，却又拿不出对策。事实上，有许多关键时刻需要的不是思虑周全，而是那么一点点行动力。这首诗很有画面感，心忧如焚的孤勇者许穆夫人，与迂腐唠叨又无计可施的官员形成对比。

卫风·硕人

硕人其颀，衣锦褧衣。齐侯之子，卫侯之妻。

东宫之妹，邢侯之姨，谭公维私。

手如柔荑，肤如凝脂。领如蝤蛴，齿如瓠犀。

螓首蛾眉，巧笑倩兮，美目盼兮。

硕人敖敖，说于农郊。四牡有骄，朱幩镳镳，

翟茀以朝。大夫夙退，无使君劳。

河水洋洋，北流活活。施罛濊濊，鳣鲔发发，

葭菼揭揭，庶姜孽孽，庶士有朅。

The Duke's Bride

The buxom lady's big and tall,
A cape o'er her robe of brocade.
Her father, brothers, husband all
Are dukes or marquis of high grade.

Like lard congealed her skin is tender,
Her fingers like soft blades of reed;
Like larva white her neck is slender,
Her teeth like rows of melon-seed,
Her forehead like a dragonfly's,
Her arched brows curved like a bow.
Ah! Dark on white her speaking eyes,
Her cheeks with smiles and dimples glow,
The buxom lady goes along;

She passes outskirts to be wed.
Four steeds run vigorous and strong,
Their bits adorned with trappings red.
Her cab with pheasant-feathered screen
Proceeds to the court in array.
Retire, officials, from the scene!
Leave duke and her without delay!

The Yellow River wide and deep
Rolls northward its jubilant way.
When nets are played out, fishes leap
And splash and throw on reeds much spray.
Richly-dressed maids and warriors keep
Attendance on her bridal day.

一

君子偕老

身材高挑的美人，穿锦绣衣裙，麻质披风加身。

她是齐侯的女儿，卫侯的妻子。

齐太子的妹妹，邢侯的小姨，谭公则是她姐妹的夫婿。

她十指纤柔，如初生白茅，肌肤似凝固的脂膏。

脖颈白皙修长如蝤蛴，牙齿像才嗑出来的瓠瓜子儿。

额广如蟓，眉弯似蛾，她笑起来酒窝荡漾，一双美目顾盼自如。

身材高挑的美人，停车在农郊。

四匹雄马仪态不凡，马嘴上装饰着华丽的朱帛。

雉羽插在车围，她端坐其中，施施然来朝。

大夫们早点退下吧，不要让你们的君主太辛劳。

河水盛大，朝北奔流。

渔网撒入河中，鳣鱼、鲔鱼蹦得欢实，芦苇与荻，密密匝匝。

陪嫁的姜家姑娘衣着华丽，护送的诸陈威武健壮。

　　诗中女子的身份，前几句讲得已经很清楚。非凡的背景，注定她的婚姻不是两个人之间的事，所以她被各种围观，被分化成一个个细节。虽然作者极尽赞叹之能事，但是，她的灵魂，她自我的需求完全被忽略了。像是被各种完美条件堆砌出来的一个工具人，不知道这巅峰时刻，她的内心是否有一丝莫名的悲凉。

王风·中谷有蓷

中谷有蓷 tuī,暵 hàn 其干矣。有女仳离,嘅其叹矣。

嘅其叹矣,遇人之艰难矣!

中谷有蓷,暵其脩矣。有女仳离,条其啸矣。

条其啸矣,遇人之不淑矣!

中谷有蓷,暵其湿矣①。有女仳离,啜其泣矣。

啜其泣矣,何嗟及矣!

Grief of a Deserted Wife

Amid the vale grow mother-worts;
They are withered and dry.
There's a woman her lord deserts.
O hear her sigh!
O hear her sigh!
Her lord's a faithless guy.

Amid the vale grow mother-worts;
They are scorched and dry.
There's a woman her lord deserts.

O hear her cry!
O hear her cry!
She has met a bad guy.

Amid the vale grow mother-worts;
They are now drowned and wet.
There's a woman her lord deserts.
See her tears jet!
See her tears jet!
It's too late to regret.

长在谷中的益母草，风吹日晒，已然干枯。
那个女子遭遇离弃，总是叹息复叹息。
叹息复叹息，遇良人何其难矣。

长在谷中的益母草，风吹日晒，已然干枯。
那个女子遭遇离弃，悲声漫长，不可聆听。
悲声漫长，遇人之不淑矣。

长在谷中的益母草，风吹日晒，已然干枯。
那个女子遭遇离弃，时常低声哭泣。
一边低声哭泣，一边叹悔不及。

　　在以男性为主导的社会，有些女人常常
通过谋爱的方式来谋生。而她们一旦被抛弃，
就意味着没有任何遮蔽地站在天地间，承受
风吹日晒，憔悴在所难免。

①湿：暵的假借字，意为"干"。

郑风·大叔于田

叔于田,乘乘马。执辔如组,两骖如舞。叔在薮,火烈具举。袒裼暴虎，

献于公所。将叔勿狃^{niǔ}，戒其伤女。

叔于田,乘乘黄。两服上襄,两骖雁行。叔在薮,火烈具扬。叔善射忌,

又良御忌。抑磬控忌,抑纵送忌。

叔于田,乘乘鸨。两服齐首,两骖如手。叔在薮,火烈具阜。叔马慢忌,

叔发罕忌。抑释掤忌,抑鬯^{chàng}弓忌。

Hunting

Our lord goes hunting in the land,
Mounted in his cab with four steeds.
He waves and weaves the reins in hand;
Two outside horses dance with speed.
Our lord goes hunting in grass land;
The hunters' torches flame in a ring.
He seizes a tiger with bared hand
And then presents it to the king.
Don't try, my lord, to do it again
For fear you may get hurt with pain!

Mounted in his chariot and four,
Hunting afield our lord does go.
The inside horses run before;
Two on the outside follow in a row.
Our lord goes to the waterside;
The hunters' torches blaze up high.
He knows not only how to ride
But also shoot with his sharp eye.
He runs and stops his steeds at will
And shoots his arrows with great skill.

Mounted in cab and four steeds fine,
Our lord goes hunting in the lands.
Two on the inside have their heads in a line;
Two on the outside follow like two hands.
To waterside our lord does go;
The hunters' fire spreads everywhere.
His grey and yellow steeds go slow;
The arrows he shoots become rare.
Aside his quiver now he lays
And returns his bow to the case.

叔去围场打猎，乘着四匹马拉的车。

他挥舞缰绳宛如丝带，两匹骖马跟着他的手势起舞。

叔就在那沼泽地旁，盛大的篝火火焰上举。

叔赤膊搏猛虎，献给公所里的爵爷。

叔啊不要掉以轻心，小心它伤到你。

叔去围场打猎，乘着四匹黄马拉的车。

中间两匹昂首向天，旁边两匹雁行向前。

叔在那沼泽地旁，盛大的篝火火焰飞扬。

叔善于射箭，又长于驾驭。

能让马儿戛然而止，也能放手让它疾行如火。

叔去围场打猎，乘着四匹花马拉的车。

中间的马匹齐头并进，两边的马匹像他左右手。

叔在那沼泽旁，篝火盛大，火焰如颤动的山丘。

叔的马匹慢下来了，叔的箭越来越少了。

叔把箭放回箭袋了，叔的弓也收回去了。

　　《毛诗序》认为这首诗"刺庄公"，大约刺庄公爱好围猎不务正业的意思。但如果是讽刺，未免过于含蓄，作为后世读者，只看到一位身手矫健、装备精良的青年猎人，奉献出一场完美的围猎秀。现代研究者则认为作者应该是"叔"的恋人，倒也不必如此坐实。这力与美的结合，无论男女老少看了都会为之所动。

郑风·清人

清人在彭，驷介旁旁。二矛重英，河上乎翱翔。

清人在消，驷介麃麃。二矛重乔，河上乎逍遥。

清人在轴，驷介陶陶。左旋右抽，中军作好。

Qing Warriors

Qing warriors stationed out,
Four mailed steeds run about.
Two spears adorned with feathers red,
Along the stream they roam ahead.

Qing warriors stationed on the shore
Look martial in their cab and four.
Two spears with pheasant's feathers red,
Along the stream they stroll ahead.

Qing warriors stationed on the stream
Look proud in their cab and mailed team.
Driver at left, spearsman at right,
The general shows his great delight.

清邑军人来守彭，马匹健壮装备精良。

染红的羽毛插在两只长矛上，在河边挥舞似翔翔。

清邑军人来守消，马匹威武装备精良。

雄雉羽毛插在两只长矛上，在河边挥舞多逍遥。

清邑军人来守轴，装备精良马匹乐陶陶。

他们忽而向左转车，忽而向右拔刀，军中统帅干得真好。

句句都像在夸赞，但只会让人感到滑稽，是讽刺无疑了。这首诗讽刺卫国将领高克带兵无方，军纪涣散，徒有形式而已。

君子偕老

郑风·羔裘

羔裘如濡，洵直且侯。彼其之子，舍命不渝。

羔裘豹饰，孔武有力。彼其之子，邦之司直。

羔裘晏兮，三英粲兮。彼其之子，邦之彦兮。

Officer in Lamb's Fur

His fur of lamb is white
As the man is upright.
The officer arises
Unchanged in a crisis.

With cuffs of leopard-skin,
The fur of lamb he's in
Makes him look strong and bold;
To the right he will hold.

His fur of lamb is bright
With three stripes left and right.
The officer stands straight,
A hero of the State.

一

君子偕老

羔羊皮袍,似有水光,穿皮袍的人,正直又美好。

他那个人啊,哪怕舍命都不会改变原则。

羔羊皮袍,用豹皮装饰,穿皮袍的人,孔武有力。

他那个人啊,在这个国家专管正人过失。

羔羊皮袍,灿烂鲜明,三道镶边,璀璨美丽。

他那个人啊,是这国中的俊杰。

　　羔羊皮袍,雍容华贵,更重要的是它温
润洁白,可以象征品格高洁。羔裘而加豹皮,
高洁之外更有一种威严。用服饰来烘托要颂
扬的对象,因为有着画面感,故而有说服力。

凤凰
于飞

第二章

CHAPTER TWO

Phoenixes fly

齐风·鸡鸣

「鸡既鸣矣，朝既盈矣。」「匪鸡则鸣，苍蝇之声。」

「东方明矣，朝既昌矣。」「匪东方则明，月出之光。」

「虫飞薨薨，甘与子同梦。」「会且归矣，无庶予子憎。」

A Courtier and His Wife

"Wake up! "she says, "Cocks crow.
The court is on the go. "
"It's not the cock that cries, "
He says, "but humming flies. "

"The east is brightening;
The court is in full swing. "
"It's not the east that's bright
But the moon shedding light. "

"See buzzing insects fly.
It's sweet in bed to lie. "
"But courtiers will not wait;
None likes you to be late. "

"雄鸡已经在报晓,朝堂上可能已经站满了人。"

"那不是鸡叫,是苍蝇嗡嗡。"

"你看东方已亮,朝堂的人越来越多了。"

"并非东方已亮,是月出之光。"

"让那虫子嗡嗡地飞,我愿与你同入梦。"

"朝堂上的大夫就要回去,不要让他们憎恶我。"

君王沉醉于温柔乡,贤妃却有很多顾忌。对话戛然而止,不知道后来的情节,只是扫了君王兴的人也许会被嘉许表彰,却很容易被更识趣的人取而代之,可以参照班婕妤的际遇。

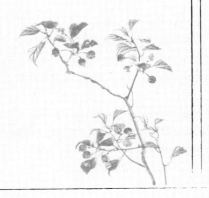

齐风·东方未明

东方未明，颠倒衣裳。颠之倒之，自公召之。

东方未晞，颠倒裳衣。倒之颠之，自公令之。

折柳樊圃，狂夫瞿瞿。不能辰夜，不夙则莫。

A Tryst before Dawn

Before the east sees dawn,
You put on clothes upside down.
O upside down you put them on,
For orders come from ducal crown.

Before the east is bright,
You take the left sleeve for the right
You put in left sleeve your right arm,
For orders bring disorder and alarm.

Don't leave my garden fence with willow tree;
Do not stare at my naked body, please.
You either come too late at night,
Or leave me early in twilight.

　　东边还未明亮，我就抓起衣裳，上衣下裳颠倒，为何如此惊慌？

　　我慌得颠倒衣裳，是因为公爷有令，叫我立即到场。

　　东边还没透亮，我就抓起衣裳，上衣下裳颠倒，为何如此惊慌？

　　我慌得穿错衣裳，是因为公爷有令，叫我立即到场。

　　菜园篱笆上折一根柳条，用来计算时辰，无奈狂夫凶悍，冲着我不停地叫嚣。

　　我再无法分清白天黑夜，只知道不是早晨就是日暮。

　　这个可怜的人，随时会被征召，在无休止的劳作中，时间变成一个没有意义的概念，难免颠三倒四。但他还在竭力挣扎，想折根柳枝，给时间一个坐标，谁想不小心又惹到一个"狂夫"。

齐风·南山

南山崔崔，雄狐绥绥。鲁道有荡，齐子由归。既曰归止，曷又怀止？

葛屦五两，冠緌双止。鲁道有荡，齐子庸止。既曰庸止，曷又从止？

蓺麻如之何？衡从其亩。取妻如之何？必告父母。既曰告止，曷又鞠止？

析薪如之何？匪斧不克。取妻如之何？匪媒不得。既曰得止，曷又极止？

Incest

The southern hill is great;
A male fox seeks his mate.
The way to Lu is plain;
Your sister with her train
Goes to wed Duke of Lu.
Why should you go there too?

The shoes are made in pairs
And strings of gems she wears.
The way to Lu is plain;
Your sister goes to reign
And wed with Duke of Lu.
Why should you follow her too?

For hemp the ground is ploughed and dressed
From north to south, from east to west.
When a wife comes to your household,
Your parents should be told.
If you told your father and mother,
Should your wife go back to her brother?

How is the firewood split?
An axe can sever it.
How can a wife be won?
With go-between it's done.
To be your wife she's vowed;
No incest is allowed.

高高南山下，雄狐慢慢走。

鲁道平又宽，齐女由此过，成为鲁侯的新娘。

既然她已经成了鲁侯的新娘，齐侯你何必再念念不忘。

葛鞋成双，冠带两条。

鲁道平又宽，齐女打这过，变成鲁侯的新娘。

既然成了你鲁侯的新娘，为什么还要让她肆意飞翔。

怎么种麻，纵横撒种在田亩。

怎么娶妻，必然要禀告父母。

既然已经告知父母，为什么还让她肆意做主？

怎么砍柴，非得凭借利斧。

怎么娶妻，非得有媒人不可。

既然已经娶回家，为什么还要这么放纵她。

文姜嫁给鲁桓公后，依然与哥哥齐襄公私通。第一段讽刺齐襄公对妹妹有不伦之念。第二三四段批评鲁桓公放纵文姜。事实上，后来鲁桓公责备文姜，文姜告知齐襄公，齐襄公竟暗杀了鲁桓公。

在将女性视为私人物品的封建社会，男性也不完全受益，像鲁桓公和武大郎这类"弱势群体"没法与妻子一别两宽，会成为感情和舆论的双重受害者。

齐风·敝笱

敝笱在梁，其鱼鲂鳏_{guān}。齐子归止，其从如云。

敝笱在梁，其鱼鲂鱮_{xù}。齐子归止，其从如雨。

敝笱在梁，其鱼唯唯。齐子归止，其从如水。

Duchess Wen Jiang of Qi

The basket is worn out
And fishes swim about.
The duchess comes with crowd,
Capricious like the cloud.

The basket is worn out;
Bream and tench swim about.

The duchess comes like flower,
Inconstant like the shower.

The basket is worn out;
Fish swim freely about.
Here comes Duke of Qi's daughter,
Changeable like water.

凤凰于飞

破鱼篓丢在鱼梁,派不上用场,鲂鱼鳏鱼鱼贯过,谁能将它们阻挡。

齐国女子回娘家,她的随从悠游如云。

破鱼篓丢在鱼梁,派不上用场,鲂鱼鳏鱼鱼贯过,谁能将它们阻挡。

齐国女子回娘家,她的随从潇洒似雨。

破鱼篓丢在鱼梁,派不上用场,鱼儿自由来去,谁能将它们阻挡。

齐国女子回娘家,她的随从自在如水。

　　宫廷八卦给民间创作者无尽的灵感,文姜是《诗经》里最经常出现的身影。这首诗的主人公还是她,谁都知道,她回娘家就是私会她哥哥齐襄公。而她丈夫鲁桓公,就成为众人眼里的破鱼篓,拦不住任何一条滑溜溜的鱼,只是一个笑话而已。

齐风·载驱

载驱薄薄，
簟茀朱鞹(kuò)。
鲁道有荡，
齐子发夕。

四骊济济，
垂辔沵沵。
鲁道有荡，
齐子岂弟①。

汶水汤汤，
行人彭彭。
鲁道有荡，
齐子翱翔。

汶水滔滔，
行人儦儦②(biāo)。
鲁道有荡，
齐子游遨。

Duke of Qi and Duchess of Lu

The duke's cab drives ahead
With screens of leather red;
The duchess starts her way
Before the break of day.

The duke's steeds run amain;
Soft looks their hanging rein.
The duchess speeds her way
At the break of the day.

The river flows along;
Travellers come in throng.
Duke and duchess meet by day
And make merry all the way.

The river's overflowed
With travellers in crowd.
Duke and duchess all day.
Make merry all the way.

车轮轻捷，碾轧地面，车上有竹车帘和朱围挡。

鲁国道路太平坦，齐国女子天不亮就出发了。

四匹黑马多健壮，柔软缰绳垂下方。

鲁国道路太平坦，齐国女子多么快乐。

汶水盛大，行人熙熙攘攘。

鲁国的道路太平坦，任这齐国女子自在翱翔。

汶水汹涌，行人如山似海。

鲁国的道路太平坦，齐国女子的步履何其逍遥。

　　不用问，这齐国女子必然是文姜了。民间女子密约私期在天未亮时出发，是想要隐藏行迹，而文姜一会儿翱翔，一会儿游逛，她早早出门不过是心太急。难怪民众讽刺鲁国的道路过于平坦，亦有讽刺鲁桓公这个丈夫形同虚设之意。

①岂弟：欢乐。②儦儦：众多。

魏风·汾沮洳

彼汾沮洳，言采其莫。彼其之子，美无度。
美无度，殊异乎公路。

彼汾一方，言采其桑。彼其之子，美如英。
美如英，殊异乎公行。

彼汾一曲，言采其藚。彼其之子，美如玉。
美如玉，殊异乎公族。

A Scholar Unknown

By riverside, alas!
A scholar gathers grass.
He gathers grass at leisure,
Careful beyond measure,
Beyond measure his grace,
Why not in a high place?

By riverside picks he
The leaves of mulberry.
Amid the leaves he towers
As brilliant as flowers.
Such brilliancy and beauty,
Why not on official duty?

By riverside he trips
To gather the ox-tips.
His virtue not displayed
Like deeply buried jade.
His virtue once appears,
He would surpass his peers.

汾水低洼处，我采羊蹄草。
但见意中人，美貌世无匹。
美貌世无匹，官员怎能及。

汾水河道旁，提篮来采桑。
但见意中人，容貌比花好。
容貌比花好，官员怎能及。

汾水弯曲处，我采泽泻草。
但见意中人，其人美如玉。
其人美如玉，官员怎能及。

　　"公路""公行""公族"都是当时的官员，
想来就像当下的公务员一样，在大众眼里自
有光环。但是，在这女子眼中，她心上人的
美貌和品格秒杀一切；当别人羡慕那些官员
的风光，她仍相信纯真的爱情。

魏风·陟岵

陟彼岵^{hù}兮，瞻望父兮。父曰：嗟！予子行

役，夙夜无已。上慎旃^{zhān}哉，犹来！无止！

陟彼屺^{qǐ}兮，瞻望母兮。母曰：嗟！予季行

役，夙夜无寐。上慎旃哉，犹来！无弃！

陟彼冈兮，瞻望兄兮。兄曰：嗟！予弟行

役，夙夜必偕。上慎旃哉，犹来！无死！

A Homesick Soldier

I climb the hill covered with grass
And look towards where my parents stay.
My father would say, "Alas!
My son's on service far away;
He cannot rest night and day.
O may he take good care
To come back and not remain there! "

I climb the hill devoid of grass
And look towards where my parents stay.
My mother would say, "Alas!
My youngest son's on service far away;
He cannot sleep well night and day.

O may he take good care
To come back and not be captive there! ”

I climb the hilltop green with grass
And look towards where my brothers stay.
My eldest brother would say,
“Alas! My youngest brother is on service far **a**way;
He stays with comrades night and day.
O may he take good care
To come back and not be killed there! ”

> 我登高坡，遥望家中老父。
>
> 好像听见他在说：
>
> 　"唉，吾儿在外服役，白天黑夜不得消停，望他当心自己，依旧归来，不要停下脚步。"
>
> 我登高坡，遥望家中母亲。
>
> 好像听见她在说：
>
> 　"唉，小儿在外服役，白天黑夜，无法入睡。愿他当心自己，依旧归来，不会弃尸战场。"
>
> 我登高冈，遥望家中兄长。
>
> 好像听见他在说：
>
> 　"唉，我弟在外服役，白天黑夜和同伴在一起。愿他当心自己，依旧归来，不会死在外乡。"

　　诗中人戍边在外，辗转迁徙，乡关万里，无法归来。他思念里生出幻觉，想象亲人们都在惦记他，有很多话要叮嘱他，并殷殷期待他归来，让他能将接下来的苦旅支撑下去。

唐风 · 无衣

岂曰无衣？七兮。不如子之衣，安且吉兮。

岂曰无衣？六兮。不如子之衣，安且燠^{yù}兮。

To His Deceased Wife

Have I no dress?
You made me seven.
I'm comfortless,
Now you're in heaven.

Have I no dress?
You made me six.
I'm comfortless
As if on pricks.

岂能说我没有衣裳？我有好几套呢。

但是不如您赐的衣服，舒适又美观啊。

岂能说我没有衣裳？我有好几套呢。

但是不如您赐的衣服，舒适又温暖啊。

"七兮""六兮"都是虚词，表示有很多。
只是终究不如您给我的好。

《红楼梦》里宁国府过年，皇帝赐了
一百两金子给他们祭祖。贾珍说，自己花再
多的钱，也不及皇帝赐的这笔钱吉利，沾恩
带福的。《史记》里韩信不肯背叛刘邦，则
说刘邦"解衣衣我，推食食我"，两者结合，
大致可以猜出诗中人物的关系，以及这首诗
表达的情感。

秦风·车邻

有车邻邻，有马白颠。未见君子，寺人之令。①

阪有漆，隰有栗。既见君子，并坐鼓瑟。今者不乐，逝者其耋。

阪有桑，隰有杨。既见君子，并坐鼓簧。今者不乐，逝者其亡。

Lord Zhong of Qin

The cab bells ring;
Dappled steeds neigh.
"Let ushers bring
In friends so gay!"

There're varnish trees uphill
And chestnuts in lowland.
Friends see Lord Zhong sit still
Beside lute-playing band.

"If we do not enjoy today,
At eighty joy will pass away."

There're mulberries uphill
And willows in lowland.
Friends see Lord Zhong sit still
Beside his music band.
"If we do not enjoy today,
We'll regret when life ebbs away."

车轮碾过地面，粼粼有声，驾车的马儿白额头。

你还没见到主人，侍人还没将你到来的消息传到内室。

山坡上种着漆树，低洼处种着枲树。

终于见到君子，并肩同坐鼓瑟。

今天我们不寻欢作乐，转眼就至耄耋。

山坡上种着桑树，低洼处种着杨树。

终于见到君子，并肩同坐鼓簧。

今天我们不寻欢作乐，将来只能孤独地奔赴死亡。

通常认为这首诗是赞美秦国国君秦仲的，撇开这个背景，诗中"及时行乐"的劝诫适用于大多数人。人生苦短，应当追欢逐乐，这个道理没错；只是时光这狡猾的家伙，任你拼尽全力，也追赶不及。

着急忙慌地快乐，最终的结果也许还是失落；倒不如像孔子那样去读书，渐入忘我境界，不知老之将至。

①寺：通"侍"，宦官。

秦风·驷驖

驷驖 tiě 孔阜，六辔在手。公之媚子，从公于狩。

① 奉时辰牡，辰牡孔硕。公曰左之，舍拔则获。

游于北园，四马既闲。辀 yóu 车鸾镳，载猃 xiǎn 歇骄。

Winter Hunting

Holding in hand six reins
Of four iron-black steeds,
Our lord hunts on the plains
With good hunters he leads.

The male and female preys
Have grown to sizes fit.

"Shoot at the left! "he says;
Their arrows go and hit.

He comes to northern park
With his four steeds at leisure;
Long and short-mouthed hounds bark
 In the carriage of pleasure.

四匹黑马，强壮如铁铸，六根辔头，挽在手中。

公爷最宠爱的那个人，陪他一起狩猎。

兽官放出一群野兽，有牝有牡，肥美健壮。

公爷下令朝左走，放箭立即有收获。

狩猎归来游北园，四匹马终得安闲。

车轮轻捷，铃儿脆响，猎狗蹲在车上，目视前方。

　　一场顺利而快乐的狩猎。公爷带上最喜
欢的人，兽官放出早就准备好的野兽，一出
手就有收获，狩猎归来还有余力去北园游览。
虽然少了一点惊心动魄，但处处都是正中下
怀。据说这首诗是赞扬秦襄公的，读下来只
觉得羡慕有余，赞扬不足。

①奉时：奉，供奉。时，此。兽官在不同季节提供不同野兽给人围猎，叫作奉时。

秦风·黄鸟

交交黄鸟，止于棘。谁从穆公？子车奄息。维此奄息，百夫之特。临其穴，惴惴其栗。彼苍者天，歼我良人！如可赎兮，人百其身！

交交黄鸟，止于桑。谁从穆公？子车仲行。维此仲行，百夫之防。临其穴，惴惴其栗。彼苍者天，歼我良人！如可赎兮，人百其身！

交交黄鸟，止于楚。谁从穆公？子车鍼虎。维此鍼虎，百夫之御。临其穴，惴惴其栗。彼苍者天，歼我良人！如可赎兮，人百其身！

Burial of Three Worthies

The golden orioles flew
And lit on jujube tree.
Who's buried with Duke Mu?
The eldest of the three.
This eldest worthy son
Could be rivaled by none.
Coming to the graveside,
Who'd not be terrified?
O good Heavens on high,
Why should the worthy die?
If he could live again,
Who not have been slain?

The golden oriole flew
And lit on mulberry.
Who's buried with Duke Mu?
The second of the three.
The second worthy son
Could be equalled by none.

Coming to the graveside,
Who'd not be terrified?
O good Heavens on high,
Why should the worthy die?
If he could live again,
Who would not have been slain?

The golden oriole flew
And lit on the thorn tree.
Who's buried with Duke Mu?
The youngest of the three.
The youngest worthy son
Could be surpassed by none.
Coming to the graveside,
Who'd not be terrified?
O good Heavens on high,
Why should the worthy die?
If he could live again,
Who would not have been slain?

黄鸟飞来飞去，拣尽寒枝，止于灌木。

谁是为秦穆公殉葬的人？子车家的奄息。

这个奄息啊，一百个人也难敌。

现在他站到自己的墓穴前，也会战栗不已。

那个老天爷啊，你要杀死我的好人！

若是能赎回他的命，我愿意死一百回。

黄鸟飞来飞去，拣尽寒枝，止于桑树。

谁是为秦穆公殉葬的人？子车家的仲行。

这个仲行，能抵挡一百猛夫。

现在他站在自己的墓穴前，也会战栗不已。

那个老天爷啊，你要杀死我的好人。

若是能赎回他的命，我愿意死一百回。

黄鸟飞来飞去，拣尽寒枝，止于荆树。

谁是为秦穆公殉葬的人？子车家的鍼虎。

这个鍼虎，能降住一百猛夫。

现在他站在自己的墓穴前，也会战栗不已。

那个老天爷啊，你要杀死我的好人，

若是能赎回他的命，我愿意死一百回。

　　《左传》记载，秦穆公去世时，让子车家的奄息、仲行、鍼虎陪葬。这三位皆是勇猛良善之人，看见自己的墓穴，也难免猛虎落泪。国人一是感念三人的政绩，二是见不得如此伤心惨烈的场景，写下这首诗哀之。

秦风·无衣

岂曰无衣？与子同袍。王于兴师，修我戈矛。

与子同仇！

岂曰无衣？与子同泽。王于兴师，修我矛戟。

与子偕作！

岂曰无衣？与子同裳。王于兴师，修我甲兵。

与子偕行！

Comradeship

Are you not battle-drest?
Let's share the plate for breast!
We shall go up the line.
Let's make our lances shine!
Your foe is mine.

Are you not battle-drest?
Let's share the coat and vest!
We shall go up the line.

Let's make our halberds shine!
Your job is mine.

Are you not battle-drest?
Let's share the kilt and the rest!
We shall go up the line.
Let's make our armour shine!
We'll march your hand in mine.

何必说没有衣服，与你同穿战袍。
君王起兵征伐，收拾好我们的戈矛。
我们一起对敌。

何必说没有衣服，与你同穿里衣。
君王起兵征伐，收拾好我们的矛戟。
我们一起行动。

何必说没有衣服，与你同穿下裳。
君王起兵征伐，收拾好我们的兵器和铠甲。
我们一起前行。

    面对战争，纠结是一种本能，所谓"无衣"
也许只是不想面对。

    然而，纠结也无益，"王于兴师"。这个"王"
有人说是周王，有人说是秦王，不管是哪个王，
他的意志都不可违抗。还不如一往无前地向
前冲，互相温暖，互相鼓劲，尝试着获得一
线生机。

陈风·株林

胡为乎株林？从夏南！匪适株林，从夏南！

驾我乘马，说于株野。乘我乘驹，朝食于株！

The Duke's Mistress

"Why are you going to the Wood?
To see the fair lady's son?"
"I'm going to its neighborhood
To see the son of the fair one."

"I'll drive to the countryside
And take a short rest there;
I'll change my horse and ride
To breakfast with the fair."

为什么他们都去株林？去找夏南。

那些人不是去株林玩，而是去找夏南。

驾着我四匹马拉的豪车，停在株野。

乘着我四匹马拉的豪车，到株林去吃早饭。

　　夏南是中国历史上作风最为豪放的女子
之一，她和陈灵公以及他的大臣孔宁、仪行
父皆有私情。奇葩的是，这三位"同情兄"（《围
城》里赵辛楣笑言同一个情人就是"同情兄"）
互相并不敌视，反倒穿着她的衣服互相打趣
取乐，甚至指着她的儿子夏徵舒，互相说像
对方。

桧风·匪风

匪风发兮，匪车偈兮。顾瞻周道，中心怛兮。

匪风飘兮，匪车嘌兮。顾瞻周道，中心吊兮。

谁能亨鱼？溉之釜鬵。谁将西归？怀之好音。

Nostalgia

The wind blows a strong blast;
The carriage's running fast.
I look to homeward, way.
Who can my grief allay?

The whirlwind blows a blast;
The cab runs wild and fast.
Looking to backward way,
Can I not pine away?

Who can boil fish?
I'll wash their boiler as they wish.
Who's going west?
Will he bring words at my request?

风声在耳边呼号,车子从眼前闪过。

我回看那条通往家乡的路,心中的忧伤无法言说。

风声在耳边旋转,车子在眼前飘远。

我回看那条通往家乡的路,心中默默将往日凭吊。

谁能够烹饪鱼鲜,我这就替他洗锅。

谁将回到西方?帮我给亲人带去消息。

　　流离失所的人站在大路上,看到车来车往,通向他回不去的故乡。古人解释为桧国人流亡在外,思乡之情无法诉诸纸笔,只有通过看大路上去他故乡的车辆排解。事实上,不管哪朝哪代的游子,但凡见到与故乡有关的事物,都会有被牵动乡愁的悸动。

曹风·下泉

冽彼下泉，浸彼苞稂。忾我寤叹，念彼周京。

冽彼下泉，浸彼苞萧。忾我寤叹，念彼京周。

冽彼下泉，浸彼苞蓍。_{shī}忾我寤叹，念彼京师。

芃芃黍苗，阴雨膏之。四国有王，郇伯劳之。

The Canal

The bushy grass drowned by
Cold water flowing down,
When I awake, I sigh
For our capital town.

The bushy plants drowned by
Cold water flowing down,
When I awake, I sigh
For our old royal town.

The southernwood drowned by
Cold water flowing down,
When I awake, I sigh
For our municipal town.

Where millet grew in spring,
Enriched by happy rain;
The state ruled by the wise king,
The toilers had their grain.

二 凤凰于飞

地下泉水凛冽奔涌，浸润稂草纵横丛生。

我午夜梦回，一声叹息，怀念昔日周朝的京城。

地下泉水凛冽奔涌，浸润蓨草铺天盖地。

我午夜梦回，一声叹息，怀念昔日周朝的京城。

地下泉水凛冽奔涌，浸润蓍草生之不息。

我午夜梦回，一声叹息，怀念昔日周朝的京城。

那时黍苗茂盛，阴雨灌溉。

四方心中有天子，这是郇伯的功劳。

　　"见证历史"很可能不是一件愉快的事。
你眼看着一个个时代在眼前消失，曾经辉煌
与荣光的城市，变得一片萧条；好像自己的
人生里有些东西，也随之枯萎了。而野草只
顾放肆生长，向你炫耀天地的无情。

　　对于诗人来说，周朝不只是一座城市，
还是一段生命，看着它没落，心中忧伤。

豳风·破斧

既破我斧，又缺我斨qiāng。周公东征，四国是皇①。

哀我人斯，亦孔之将。

既破我斧，又缺我锜。周公东征，四国是吪②。

哀我人斯，亦孔之嘉。

既破我斧，又缺我銶qiú。周公东征，四国是遒③。

哀我人斯，亦孔之休。

With Broken Axe

With broken axe in hand
And hatchet, our poor mates
Follow our duke from eastern land;
We've conquered the four States.
Alas! Those who are not strong
Cannot come along.

With broken axe in hand
And chisel, our poor mates
Follow our duke from eastern land;
We've controlled the four States.
Alas! Those who do not survive!
Lucky those still alive.

With broken axe in hand
And halberd, our poor mates
Follow our duke from eastern land
We've ruled o'er the four States.
Alas! Those who are dead!
Lucky, let's go ahead.

使破了我的斧子，又残缺了我的**斨**。
周公东征，四方得到匡正。
感叹我们这些百姓，也算是有幸。

使破了我的斧子，又残缺了我的**锜**。
周公东征，四方得到教化。
感叹我们这些百姓，运气不能算不好啊。

使破了我的斧子，又残缺了我的**銶**。
周公东征，从此四方得以稳定。
感叹我们这些百姓，就要见到光明。

　　斨、锜、銶都是农耕用具，使用到残破，
可见百姓何其辛劳。周公东征，天下太平。
对于普通百姓来说，最实惠的就是不用给多
个统治者交税。这首诗中对周公的期待，也
不完全是愚忠，而是生存本能使然。

①皇：匡，正。②吪：教化。③遒：坚固，安定。

高山×仰止

第三章

CHAPTER THREE

You're good like mountains high

鹿鸣之什·四牡

四牡骓骓，周道倭迟。岂不怀归？王事靡盬(gǔ)，我心伤悲。

四牡骓骓，啴啴(tān)骆马。岂不怀归？王事靡盬，不遑启处。

翩翩者鵻，载飞载下，集于苞栩。王事靡盬，不遑将父。

翩翩者鵻，载飞载止，集于苞杞。王事靡盬，不遑将母。

驾彼四骆，载骤骎骎(qīn)。岂不怀归？是用作歌，将母来谂。

Loyalty and Filial Piety

Four horses forward go
Along a winding way.
How can my homesickness not grow?
But the king's affairs bear no delay.
My heart is full of woe.

Four horses forward go;
They pant and snort and neigh.
How can my homesickness not grow?
But the king's affairs bear no delay.
I can't rest nor drive slow.

Doves fly from far and near
Up and down on their way.
They may rest on oaks with their peer.
But the king's affairs bear no delay,
And I can't serve my father dear.

Doves fly from far and near
High and low on their way.
They may perch on trees with their peer.
But the king's affairs bear no delay,
And I can't serve my mother dear.

I drive black-maned white steed
And hurry on my way.
Don't I wish to go home with speed?
I can't but sing this lay
Though I have my mother to feed.

三

高山仰止

*

四马奔驰，道路曲折漫长。

岂不怀归？公事无休止，我心伤悲。

四马奔驰，白马喘息不已。

岂不怀归？公事无休止，哪有空歇？

斑鸠翩飞，忽下忽上，忽然立于柞树。

公事无休止，我顾不上我的老父。

斑鸠翩飞，忽起忽止，忽然立于杞树。

公事无休止，我顾不上我的老娘。

四匹白马拉着车，马蹄哒哒，车轮飞快。

我何尝不想回到故里，所以写下这首歌，将我的母亲来思念。

此诗像是一个出差在外的小公务员写给亲人的家书。全诗在"王事靡盬"与"岂不怀归"的矛盾中展现了主人公伤悲的感情世界。此诗虽是发泄牢骚，不满"王事靡盬"之作，但也可被曲解成忠孝不能两全而勉力尽忠王事之作，所以统治者用此诗来慰劳使臣的风尘劳顿。

鹿鸣之什·皇皇者华

皇皇者华，于彼原隰。駪駪征夫，每怀靡及。

我马维驹，六辔如濡。载驰载驱，周爰咨诹。

我马维骐，六辔如丝。载驰载驱，周爰咨谋。

我马维骆，六辔沃若。载驰载驱，周爰咨度。

我马维骃，六辔既均。载驰载驱，周爰咨询。

The Envoy

The flowers look so bright
On lowland and on height.
The envoy takes good care
To visit people here and there.

"My ponies have brown manes
 And smooth are the six reins.
I ride them here and there,
Making inquiries everywhere. "

"My horses have white manes;
Silken are the six reins.
I ride them here and there,
Seeking counsel everywhere. "

"My horses have black manes;
Glossy are the six reins.
I ride them here and there,
Seeking advice everywhere. "

"My horses have grey manes;
Shiny are the six reins.
I ride them here and there,
Visiting people everywhere. "

高山仰止

花开如锦，在原野的低洼处。

那许多出使在外的人，总担心有许多事做不周全。

我的马都是骏马，六根缰绳闪烁光泽。

驾着马车朝前赶，上面交给我的事，我都要寻访分明。

我的马都是骏马，六根缰绳如丝毂光滑。

驾着马车朝前赶，上面交给我的事，我要了解而且考虑清楚。

我的马都是骏马，六根缰绳柔软而润泽。

驾着马车朝前赶，上面交给我的事，我要了解再和大家商量。

我的马都是骏马，六根缰绳用力均匀。

带着马车朝前赶，上面交给我的事，我要了解然后追问后续。

　　此诗是奉王命出使在外的人的独白。他自知责任重大，深恐不够周全，要深入了解，思考周密，和大家商量对策，还要追问结果。此诗写尽使臣的风尘仆仆和殚思竭虑。

鹿鸣之什·天保

天保定尔，亦孔之固。俾尔单厚^①，何福不除？俾尔多益，以莫不庶。

天保定尔，俾尔戬^②谷。罄无不宜，受天百禄。降尔遐福，维日不足。

天保定尔，以莫不兴。如山如阜，如冈如陵，如川之方至，以莫不增。

吉蠲（juān）为饎（chì），是用孝享。禴（yuè）祠烝尝，于公先王。君曰：卜尔，万寿无疆。

神之吊矣，诒尔多福。民之质矣，日用饮食。群黎百姓，遍为尔德。

如月之恒，如日之升。如南山之寿，不骞不崩。如松柏之茂，无不尔或承。

The Royalty

May Heaven bless our king
With great security,
Give him favor and bring
Him great felicity
That he may do more good
And people have more food.

May Heaven bless our king
With perfect happiness,
Make him do everything.
Right and with great success
That he may have his will
And we enjoy our fill.

May Heaven bless our king
With great prosperity
Like hills and plains in spring
Grown to immensity
Or the o'erbrimming river
Flowing forever and ever.

Offer your wine and rice
From summer, fall to spring
As filial sacrifice
To your ancestral king
Whose soul in the witch appears:
"May you live long, long years!"

The spirit comes and confers
Many blessings on you
And on simple laborers
But daily food and brew
The common people raise
Their voice to sing your praise:

"Like the moon in the sky
Or sunrise o'er the plain,
Like southern mountains high
Which never fall or wane
Or like luxuriant pines,
May such be your succeeding lines!"

上天保佑这天下安宁，您的江山永固。

让您应有尽有，什么福气会不给您？

使您有诸多财富，怎么可能不富庶？

上天保佑这天下安宁，给您无尽福禄。

所有的事都合适，您安享天赐的百禄。

降给您的福气至无穷远，不要担心光阴匆促，
时日不足。

上天保佑这天下安宁，每一个角落都繁茂兴盛。

就像山岭隆起，丘陵顶天立地，百川到海，绝
不会有减无增。

在吉日清洗酒食，孝敬祖宗与众神。

一年四季祭祀不断，供奉先公先王。

祭司代传先君之语：赐你，这万寿无疆。

诸神降临，赐您多福。

民风质朴，日用饮食周全。

从上到下，无不感激您的恩德。

您就像月亮逐渐圆满，您就像太阳冉冉上升。

您寿比南山，永远不会有任何事，对您有所损伤。

您就像松柏之茂盛。这一切，您的儿孙也完全
继承。

此诗是大臣祝颂君主的颂诗，一再强调他的福气是老天赐予。他与上天沟通的方式是祭祀，他可与上天直接对话，这就使得他有了某种不可取代性。

①单厚：《毛诗传笺通释》：单、厚同义，皆为大也。②戬穀：戬，福。穀，禄。

南有嘉鱼之什·蓼萧

蓼彼萧斯，零露湑兮。既见君子，我心写兮。燕笑语兮，是以有誉处兮。

蓼彼萧斯，零露瀼瀼。既见君子，为龙为光。其德不爽，寿考不忘。

蓼彼萧斯，零露泥泥。既见君子，孔燕岂弟。宜兄宜弟，令德寿岂①。

蓼彼萧斯，零露浓浓。既见君子，鞗革忡忡。和鸾雍雍，万福攸同。

Southernwood

How long grows southernwood
With dew on it so bright!
Now I see my men good,
My heart is glad and light.
We talk and laugh and feast;
Of our care we are eased.

How high grows southernwood
With heavy dew so bright!
Now we see our lord good
Like dragon and sunlight.
With impartiality
He'll enjoy longevity.

How green grows southernwood
Wet with fallen dew bright!
Now I see my men good.
Let us feast with delight
And enjoy brotherhood,
Be happy day and night.

How sweet the southernwood
In heavy dew does stand!
Now we see our lord good,
Holding the reins in hand.
Bells ringing far and near,
We're happy without peer.

　　艾蒿草长得高高的，露珠正在溅落。

　　我见到周天子，心里别提多舒畅。

　　欢宴，谈笑，这是我开心的所在。

　　艾蒿草长得高高的，露珠闪烁光芒。

　　我见到周天子，这是恩宠也是光荣。

　　他的德行分毫不差，必将万寿无疆。

　　艾蒿草长得高高的，露珠润泽明亮。

　　我见到周天子，他平易近人我们相处甚欢。

　　像是兄长又像是弟弟，拥有美德的人会长寿
快乐。

　　艾蒿草长得高高的，露珠紧密相拥。

　　我见到周天子，他马儿的缰绳低垂。

　　车上的铃儿叮当，愿世间幸福从天而降，都落
入他的怀中。

这是一首典型的祝颂诗，表达了诸侯朝见周天子时的尊崇和歌颂之意。周天子宴请诸侯，诸侯向他表示感激；露水象征着天子的福泽，多而明亮，润泽了用艾蒿草形容的诸侯。

①寿岂：寿恺。恺，快乐。

南有嘉鱼之什·彤弓

彤弓弨^{chāo}兮，受言藏之。我有嘉宾，中心贶之。
钟鼓既设，一朝飨之。
彤弓弨兮，受言载之。我有嘉宾，中心喜之。
钟鼓既设，一朝右之。
彤弓弨兮，受言櫜^{gāo}①之。我有嘉宾，中心好之。
钟鼓既设，一朝酬②之。

The Red Bow

Receive the red bow unbent
And have it stored.
It's a gift I present
To guest adored.
Drums beat and bells ring soon.
Let's feast till noon.

Receive the red bow unbent
Fitt'd on its frame.
It's a gift I present
To guest of fame.
Drums beat and bells ring soon.
Let's drink till noon.

Receive the red bow unbent
Placed in its case.
It's a gift I present
To guest with grace.
Drums beat and bells ring soon.
Let's eat till noon.

高山仰止

红色的弓，弦已放松，请接受并收藏。
我有嘉宾，情之所钟。
钟鼓乐器已摆好，在这一天请享受。

红色的弓，弦已放松，请接受并收藏。
我有嘉宾，情之所钟。
钟鼓乐器已摆好，在这一天就听我劝酒。

红色的弓，弦已放松，请接受并收藏。
我有嘉宾，情之所钟。
钟鼓乐器已经摆好，在这一天里觥筹交错。

　　《毛诗序》说，这首诗是"天子锡有功
诸侯也"，将弓弦放松之后赐给诸侯，表示
这一天无须紧张，可以畅快饮酒欢乐。表面
看是周天子为有功的诸侯庆功，实际上是歌
颂周天子的文治武功。

①右：通"侑"，劝酒。②酬：互相敬酒。

鴥彼飞隼，其飞戾天，亦集爰止。方叔莅止，

其车三千。师干之试，方叔率止。钲人伐鼓，

陈师鞠旅。显允方叔，伐鼓渊渊，振旅阗阗。

蠢尔蛮荆，大邦为雠。方叔元老，克壮其犹。

方叔率止，执讯获丑。戎车啴啴，啴啴焞焞，

如霆如雷。显允方叔，征伐玁狁，蛮荆来威。

General Fang

Let's gather millet white
In newly broken land.
General Fang will alight
Here to take the command.
Three thousand cars arrive
With his great well trained forces.
The general takes a drive
On four black and white horses.
Four piebalds in a row
Draw chariot red and green,
With reins and hooks aglow
Seal skin and bamboo screen.

Let's gather millet white
In newly broken land.
General Fang will alight
On the field rein in hand.
Three thousand cars arrive
With flags and banners spread.
The general leads the drive
In chariot painted red.
Hear eight bells' tinkling sound
And gems of pendant ring.
See golden girdle round
His robe conferred by the king.

三 高山仰止

南有嘉鱼之什·采芑

薄言采芑，于彼新田，于此菑亩。方叔莅止，

其车三千。师干之试，方叔率止。乘其四骐，

四骐翼翼。路车有奭①，簟茀鱼服②，钩膺鞗革。

薄言采芑，于彼新田，于此中乡。方叔莅止，

其车三千。旂旐央央，方叔率止。约𫐄错衡，

八鸾玱玱。服其命服，朱芾斯皇，有玱葱珩。

Rapid is the hawks' flight:
They soar up to the sky
And then here they alight.
General Fang comes nigh;
Three thousand cars arrive;
His well-trained soldiers come.
General Fang leads the drive;
Men ingle and beat drum
His forces in array,
The general has good fame,
Drums rolling on display
And flags streaming in flame.

You southern savages dare
To invade our great land.
Our General Fang is there;
At war he's a good hand.
The general leads his forces
To make captives of the crowd.
His chariot drawn by horses
Now rumbles now rolls loud
Like clap or roll of thunder.
General Fang in command
Puts the Huns down and under
And southern savage band.

　　我采苦菜，在那开垦了两年的新田，在这刚开垦的田亩间。

　　方叔到来，战车三千。众人捍卫国土，方叔带他们上战场。

　　他的车子四匹花马来拉，花马脚步齐刷刷。

　　赤色战车多醒目，车上竹帘镶兽皮，马身饰带皮缰绳。

　　我采苦菜，在那开垦了两年的新田，在这块田的中间。

　　方叔到来，战车三千。

　　龟蛇旗色泽鲜明，方叔带他们上战场。

　　车毂横木精装饰，八只鸾铃响锵锵。

　　方叔官服穿在身，赤色蔽膝辉煌，葱玉轻叩**玱玱**。

　　隼鸟疾飞，直上苍天，忽然落下。

　　方叔到来，战车三千。

　　众人捍卫国土，方叔领他们上战场。

　　擂响战鼓，列队训诫兵士。

　　了不起的方叔，击鼓声渊渊，训练兵士的声音阗阗。

　　愚蠢的蛮荆，与我大邦为仇。

　　方叔这元老，能拿出奇谋。

　　方叔率领战士上战场，讯问俘虏。

　　兵车响嘽嘽，这嘽嘽声恢宏，如霆如雷。

　　了不起的方叔，征伐猃狁，威震蛮荆。

　　周宣王时，派方叔征荆蛮。这首诗通过
战车的外形、声响和方叔的着装等，写出大
军必胜的气势。研究者通常认为，这是出征
前的祝福之诗。

①奭：赤色。②鱼：有兽名鱼。③焞焞：盛大。

南有嘉鱼之什·车攻

我车既攻，我马既同。四牡庞庞，驾言徂东。田车既好，四牡孔阜。东有

甫草，驾言行狩。

之子于苗①，选徒嚣嚣。建旐设旄，搏兽于敖②。驾彼四牡，四牡奕奕。赤芾

金舄，会同有绎。

③决拾既伙，弓矢既调。射夫既同，助我举柴。四黄既驾，两骖不猗。不失

其驰，舍矢如破。

萧萧马鸣，悠悠旆旌。徒御不惊，大庖不盈。之子于征，有闻无声。允矣

君子，展也大成。

Great Hunting

Our chariots strong
Have well-matched steeds.
Our train is long;
Eastward it seeds.
Our chariots good,
Four steeds in front,
Drive to east wood
Where we shall hunt.

Our king afield,
Flags on display,
With archers skilled
Pursues his prey.
He drives four steeds
Strong and aglow.
Red-shoed, he leads
His lords in row.

Strings fit, they choose
Arrows and bows.
Archers in twos
Reap games in rows.
Four yellow steeds
Run straight and fit.
Our chariot speeds,
Each shot a hit.

Long, long steeds neigh;
Flags float and stream.
Footmen look gay;
With smiles cooks beam.
On backward way.
We hear no noise.
What happy day! How we rejoice!

*

我的车已经坚固，我的马已经聚齐。

四匹公马强壮，驾着猎车往东。

猎车是上等货色，四匹公马威猛。

东边有那大草泽，驾车前去狩猎。

那个人要去夏猎，挑选随从大家齐作声。

竖起一杆杆牛尾旗，狩猎在那敖地。

四匹公马拉着车，四匹公马高大。

赤色蔽膝金靴子，同好陆陆续续到来。

有扳指，也有护臂，调至最佳状态的是弓矢。

射夫们同心协力，帮我捡回打猎的成绩。

四匹黄马驾车出发，不偏不倚是两匹骖马。

御者走得很有章法，放出去的箭总能中靶。

耳听马鸣声萧萧，眼望旄旗悠悠飘。

士卒与马夫机警，大厨不让食物过剩。

那个人狩猎归来，你听到消息但悄然无声。

有诚信的君子，确实军纪严明。

　　周宣王会同诸侯夏猎，场面宏伟，气势磅礴，也是展现武力的一种方式。另外，通过严明军纪，展现了周宣王威震四方的文治武功。

①苗：夏猎。②搏兽：假借字。"薄狩"，薄是发语词。③决拾：决，扳指。拾：护臂。

鸿雁之什·庭燎

夜如何其？夜未央，庭燎之光。
君子至止，鸾声将将。

夜如何其？夜未艾，庭燎晣晣。zhé
君子至止，鸾声哕哕。

夜如何其？夜乡晨，庭燎有辉。
君子至止，言观其旂。

Early Audience

How goes the night?
It's at its height.
In royal court a hundred torches blaze bright.
Before my lords appear,
Their ringing bells I'll hear.

How goes the night?
It's passed its height.
In royal court the torches shed a lambent light.
Before my lords appear,
Their tinkling bells will come near.

How goes the night?
Morning is near.
In royal court is blown out torches' light.
Now all my lords appear;
I see their banners from here.

夜有几分？

夜还未尽，您看到的，是庭院里火炬的光。

诸侯就要到了，您听那鸾铃叮叮当当。

夜有几分？

夜还未尽。您看到的，是庭院里火炬的光。

诸侯就要到了，您听那鸾铃越来越响。

夜有几分？夜色尽露晨光。

庭院里，火炬尚且有光辉。

诸侯就要到了，可以看到那龙旗已经临近。

《毛诗序》称此诗赞美宣王翘首期待诸
侯来朝，表现出他勤于国事、体恤臣下的情怀。
这是一篇赞美君王勤于朝政的颂诗。

鸿雁之什·祈父

祈父^①，予王之爪牙。胡转予于恤，
靡所止居？

祈父，予王之爪士。胡转予于恤，
靡所厎止？

祈父，亶不聪。胡转予于恤？
有母之尸饔^②。

To the Minister of War

O minister of war!
We're soldiers of the crown.
Why send us to an expeditionary corps
So that we cannot settle down?

O minister of war!
We're guardians' of this land.
Why send us to an expeditionary corps
So that we're under endless command?

O minister of war!
Why don't you listen to others?
Why send us to an expeditionary corps
So that we cannot feed out mothers?

司马，我是守护王的爪牙。

为何把我调往可忧之地？让我居无定所。

司马，我是守护王的武二。

为何把我调到可忧之地？让我有家难至。

司马，你实在是个蠢货！

为何把我调到可忧之地？家中老母吃不上一口热饭。

　　《诗经》里有各种各样的牢骚。这首描述的是本该保卫王室的武士，对司马派遣到远方战场的斥责。武士无法接受，从责备到怒骂，直抒胸臆，体现了武士心直口快，敢怒敢言的性格特征。

①祈父：即"圻父"。职掌都城禁卫的长官，即司马。②尸饔：尸，通"失"。饔，熟食。

鸿雁之什·无羊

谁谓尔无羊？三百维群。谁谓尔无牛？九十其犉。尔羊来思，其角濈濈 ^{ji}。尔牛来思，其耳湿湿。

或降于阿，或饮于池，或寝或讹。尔牧来思，何蓑何笠，或负其餱。三十维物，尔牲则具。

尔牧来思，以薪以蒸，以雌以雄。尔羊来思，矜矜兢兢，不骞不崩。麾之以肱，毕来既升。

牧人乃梦，众维鱼矣，旐维旟矣。大人占之：众维鱼矣，实维丰年；旐维旟矣，室家溱溱。

The Herdsmen's Song

Who says you have no sheep?
There're three hundred in herd.
Have you no cows to keep?
Ninety cattle's low is heard.
Your sheep don't strive for corn;
They're at peace horn to horn.
When your cattle appears,
You see their frapping ears.

Some cattle go downhill;
Others drink water clear.
Some move; others lie still.
When your herdsmen appear,
They bear hats of bamboos
And carry food and rice.
Cattle of thirty hues
Are fit for sacrifice.

Then come your men of herds
With large and small firewood
And male and female birds.
Your sheep appear so good;
Fat, they don't run away;
Tame, they don't go astray.
At wave of arms, behold!
They come back to the fold.

Then dreams the man of herds
Of locusts turned to fishes.
Tortoise and snake to birds.
The witch divines our wishes:
The locust turned to fish
Foretells a bumper year;
The snakes turned, as we wish,
To greater household dear.

谁说你没有羊？三百成一群。

谁说你没有牛？大牛九十头。

你的羊来了，羊角儿聚在一起。

你的牛来了，一大片耳朵摇摇。

　　它们或走下山丘，或饮水于池塘，或者睡觉，或者动个不停。

　　你的牧人来了，披着蓑衣戴着斗笠，背着各种粮草。

　　牛羊毛色那么多，各色祭牲都具备。

　　你的牧人来了，粗柴细草全部有，雌牲雄畜皆齐全。

　　你的羊奔过来了，战战兢兢，唯恐落单，不会损减，绝不会溃散。

　　牧人挥动手臂，它们齐齐入了羊圈。

　　牧人做了梦，所有蝗虫都变成鱼，龟蛇旗变成隼鸟旗。

　　太卜帮他解梦，蝗虫变成鱼，实在是丰年的征兆。

　　龟蛇旗变成隼鸟旗，这个家必人丁兴旺乐陶陶。

　　《毛诗序》曰："《无羊》，宣王考牧
也。"周厉王时，牧业几乎荒废。到周宣王时，
再次大力发展牧业。这首诗赞扬牛羊成群的
盛况，描摹精妙，笔底蕴情，达到了极高的
艺术境界。

则无膴仕。

昊天不佣，降此鞠讻。昊天不惠，降此大戾。君子如届，俾民心阕。君子如夷，

恶怒是违。

不吊昊天，乱靡有定。式月斯生，俾民不宁。忧心如酲，谁秉国成？不自为政，

卒劳百姓。

驾彼四牡，四牡项领。我瞻四方，蹙蹙靡所骋。

方茂尔恶，相尔矛矣。既夷既怿，如相酬矣。

昊天不平，我王不宁。不惩其心，覆怨其正。

家父作诵，以究王讻。式讹尔心，以畜万邦。

节南山之什·节南山

节彼南山，维石岩岩。赫赫师尹，民具尔瞻。忧心如惔，不敢戏谈。国既卒斩，

何用不监！

节彼南山，有实其猗。赫赫师尹，不平谓何。天方荐瘥，丧乱弘多。民言无嘉，

憯莫惩嗟。①

尹氏大师，维周之氐；秉国之钧，四方是维。天子是毗，俾民不迷。不吊昊天，

不宜空我师。

弗躬弗亲，庶民弗信。弗问弗仕，勿罔君子。式夷式已，无小人殆。琐琐姻亚，

To Grand Master Yin

South Mountain's high;
Crags and jags tower.
Our people's eye
Looks to your power.
We're in distress
For state affair.
It's in a mess.
Why don't you care?

South Mountain's high,
Rugged here and there.
In people's eye:
You're as unfair.
Distress and woes
Fall without end.
Our grievance grows;
But you won't mend.

Master Yin stands
Pillar of state.
With power in hands
You rule our fate.
On you rely
People and crown.
Heaven on high!
You've false renown.

Is what you do
Worthy of trust?
We don't think you
Have used men just.
You put the mean
In a high place.
Let all your kin
Fall in disgrace!

Heaven unfair

And pitiless
Sends man to scare;
We're in distress.
Send us men just
To bring us rest,
Worthy of trust;
We're not distressed.

Great Heaven, lo!
Troubles ne'er cease.
Each month they grow;
We have no peace.
We're grieved at heart.
Who rule and reign,
Distress and nees
State set apart?
We toil with pain.

I drive my four
Steeds in harness.
I look before.
And see distress.

On evil day.
You wield your spear.
When you are gay,
You drink with cheer.

Heaven's unjust;
Our king's no rest.
To our disgust
Alone you're blest.

I sing to lay
Evil deeds bare
So that you may
Mind state affair.

南山高耸，有石磊磊。

威风的尹太师，老百姓可都在望着你。

大家忧心如焚，不敢说笑。

国运即将衰落，你却视而不见。

南山高耸，斜坡宽广。

威风的尹太师，你为什么如此不公？

上天正要降灾，举目皆是丧乱。

老百姓说起你就没好话，你从不曾将自己反观。

了不起的尹太师，你原本应该是周朝的柱石。

手握国家政权，四方安宁要你维持。

天子依靠你，百姓有了你才不会迷失。

可是上天不仁，降下这样坑人的太师。

太师你从不躬身亲为，老百姓怎么信你？

你不咨询不任用，让君子怎能不受委屈？

你不制止不打击，让小人怎能停下来？

你那些乱七八糟的裙带亲，倒是个个当着肥差。

上天不公，降下这样的灾难。

上天不善，降下这样的祸害。

君子若能到来，老百姓心里才能安生。

君子办事公正，怨气才能够消除。

上天不仁，这乱世何时能平定？

月月有灾，老百姓不得安宁。

我心忧像是饮酒醉，谁能够管好国政？

肉食者自己管不好国政，最后辛苦百姓。

我驾着四匹牡马，马儿脖颈粗壮。

我朝四方望去，天地逼仄，无路可走。

当你心中的恶蓬勃生长，不如先看看你手中的矛。

也许就会心平气和，像是在酒桌上酬唱。

苍天不平，我王不宁。

尹太师你毫无反省，还怨恨正直之人。

家父作诗讽诵，追究王朝祸乱的根本。

希望你能洗心革面，让天下万民休养生息。

　　"家父"是作者的名字。他作这首诗，旨在批评"尹太师"是国家的祸根。但历来注释者都认为，他真正批评的对象是周幽王。毕竟，这个才是有能力让天下不得安宁的"关键人物"。

①僭：曾经。

谓山盖卑，为冈为陵。民之讹言，宁莫之惩。召彼故老，讯之占梦。具曰予圣，

谁知乌之雌雄！

谓天盖高，不敢不局。谓地盖厚，不敢不蹐。维号斯言，有伦有脊。哀今之人，

胡为虺蜴？

瞻彼阪田，有菀其特。天之扤我，如不我克。彼求我则，如不我得。执我仇仇，

亦不我力。

心之忧矣，如或结之。今兹之正，胡然厉矣？燎之方扬，宁或灭之？赫赫宗周，

褒姒灭之！

节南山之什·正月

正月繁霜，我心忧伤。民之讹言，亦孔之将。念我独兮，忧心京京。哀我小心，瘅忧以痒。

父母生我，胡俾我瘉？不自我先，不自我后。好言自口，莠言自口。忧心愈愈，是以有侮。

忧心惸惸，念我无禄。民之无辜，并其臣仆。哀我人斯，于何从禄？瞻乌爰止？于谁之屋？

瞻彼中林，侯薪侯蒸。民今方殆，视天梦梦。既克有定，靡人弗胜。有皇上帝，伊谁云憎？

终其永怀，又窘阴雨。其车既载，乃弃尔辅。载输尔载，将伯助予！

无弃尔辅，员于尔辐。屡顾尔仆，不输尔载。终逾绝险，曾是不意。

鱼在于沼，亦匪克乐。潜虽伏矣，亦孔之炤。忧心惨惨，念国之为虐！

彼有旨酒，又有嘉肴。洽比其邻，昏姻孔云。念我独兮，忧心殷殷。

佌佌彼有屋，蔌蔌方有谷。民今之无禄，天夭是椓。哿矣富人，哀此惸独。

Lamentation

In frosty moon
My heart is grieved.
Rumors spread soon
Can't be believed.
I stand alone;
My grief won't go.
With cares I groan
And ill I grow.

Why wasn't I born
Before or after?
I sufer scorn
From people's laughter.
Good words or bad
Are what they say.
My heart feels sad,
Filled with dismay.

My heart feels grieved;
Unlucky am I.
People deceived,
Slaves and maids cry.
Alas for me!
Can I be blest?
The crow I see,
Where can it rest?

See in the wood
Branch large or small.
For livelihood
We sufer all.
Dark is the sky.

Who'll make it clear?
Heavens on high
Cause hate and fear.

The hills said low.
Are mountains high.
Why don't we go
Against the lie?
About our dream,
What do they know?
Though wise they seem
They can't tell male
From female crow,
To what avail?

High are the skies;
Down I must bow.
Thick the earth lies;
I must walk slow.
Though what I say
Has no mistakes,
Men of today
Bite me like snakes.

See rugged field
Where lush grows grain.
How can I yield
To might and main?
I was sought after
But couldn't be got.
With pride and laughter
They use me not.

Laden with cares,
My heart seems bound.
The state affairs.
In woe are drowned.
The flames though high
May be put out.
The world's lost by
Fair Lady Bao.

Long grieved my heart,
I meet hard rain.
Loaded your cart,
No wheels remain.
O'erturned 'twill lie;
For help you'd cry.

Keep your wheel-aid
And spoke well-made.
Show oft concern
For driver good
Lest he o'erturn.
Your cart of wood.

You may get o'er.
Difficulties,
But not before

You thought of this.
Fish in the pool
Knows no delight.
Deep in water cool
They're still in sight.

Saddened, I hate
Evils of the state.
They have' wine sweet
And viands good,
So they can treat
Their kin and neighborhood.
In loneliness I feel distress.

The poor have houses small;
Their food is coarse.
Woes on them fall;
They've no resource.
Happy the rich class;
But the poor, alas!

四月下着繁霜，我心中忧伤。

民间流言游走，传得越来越远。

我是这样一个孤独的人，忧愁萦绕我心。

可怜我总是小心翼翼，将忧烦做成了病根。

父母啊生下我，为什么使我受这么多伤？

为什么不将我生得早一点或晚一点？偏偏踩上乱世的节点。

好话出自那些口，坏话也出自那些口。

我想起来就好生担忧，反倒因此招来侮辱。

忧心无尽，想起我命小福薄。

小民何其无辜，连累我的奴仆。

可怜我这个人，到哪里能找到福分？

你看乌鸦降落，会在谁的房屋？

且看那树林里，有粗干也有细枝。

小民如今在苦难里，举头望天天也昏昏。

假如一切都有定数，没人能胜天半子。

那么皇天上帝啊，到底谁是让你憎恨的人？

谁说山不高？明明那山岗高耸。

民间的谣言，为什么不会被严惩？

请来老人，请他们帮我占梦。

他们都说自己最高明，像乌鸦难辨雌雄。

都说那天很高，但走在下面不敢不弯腰。

都说地很厚，但踩在上面不敢不小心。

人们呼喊出这样的话，确实很有道理。

悲哀的是如今世上的人，为什么宁可做毒蛇？

那山坡上的田地，有草特别繁茂。

老天真能折腾我，好像一定要把我摁倒。

当初朝廷求我去，像是生怕得不到。

求到又将我丢到一边，好像完全不需要。

我心中烦忧，如同绳子打了结。

当今朝政，为何如此暴戾？

那火焰刚刚燃起？谁能将它熄灭？

赫赫煊煊的周朝，要由褒姒灭掉。

我心中常怀忧伤，又被阴雨围困。

你车上装了东西，却将车厢板扔掉。

等到东西掉下来，又喊大哥来帮我。

不要扔掉车厢板，应该加固你的车辐。

要经常盯着你的车夫，免得掉下车上的货物。

这样才能最终逾越险境，而你对这些都不以为意。

鱼游在池沼，并不快乐的样子。

纵然潜伏在水底，对现实依然十分明了。

我忧心忡忡，想起这国家正在经受灾难。

他们有美酒，又有佳肴。

邻居相处融洽，亲戚们往来热络。

想起我独自一人，难免忧心殷殷。

宵小之辈也有屋，猥琐之人拿俸禄。

唯有百姓没福气，天降横祸常被暴击。

那些富人多么快乐，可怜的是我这孤独的人。

　　作者应为周朝官员，望着礼崩乐坏，心
中忧愤。但他也不是能够挺身而出、无私忘
我的仁人志士，所以只能够默默担忧。就算
这小心翼翼的担忧，还是给他带来麻烦，使
他被其他人耻笑侮辱。作者是这世间最为痛
苦的一类人，既不能麻木，也不肯恣睢；看
着别人在这样纷乱的世道里寻欢作乐，他只
能将孤独咬碎，承受那艰深的苦涩。

①正月：夏历四月。

抑此皇父，岂曰不时？胡为我作，不即我谋？彻我墙屋，田卒污莱。曰予不戕，礼则然矣。

皇父孔圣，作都于向。择三有事，亶侯多藏。不慭遗一老，俾守我王。择有车马，以居徂向。

黾勉从事，不敢告劳。无罪无辜，谗口嚣嚣。下民之孽，匪降自天。噂沓背憎，职竞由人。②

悠悠我里，亦孔之痗。四方有羡，我独居忧。民莫不逸，我独不敢休。天命不彻，我不敢效我友自逸。③

节南山之什 · 十月之交

十月之交，朔月辛卯。日有食之，亦孔之丑。彼月而微，此日而微；今此下民，

亦孔之哀。

于何不臧。

日月告凶，不用其行。四国无政，不用其良。彼月而食，则维其常；此日而食，

胡憯莫惩？

烨烨震电，不宁不令。百川沸腾，山冢崒崩。高岸为谷，深谷为陵。哀今之人，

皇父卿士，番维司徒。家伯维宰，仲允膳夫。棸子内史，蹶维趣马。楀维师氏，

艳妻煽方处。

President Huang Fu

In the tenth month the sun and moon
Cross each other on the first day.
The sun was then eclipsed at noon,
An evil omen, people say.
The moon became then small;
The sun became not bright.
The people one and all.
Are in a wretched plight.

Bad omen, moon and sun
Don't keep their proper way.
In the states evil's done;
The good are kept away.
The eclipse of the moon
Is not uncommon thing;
That of the sun at noon
Will dire disaster bring.

Lightning flashes, rolls thunder,
There is nor peace nor rest.
The streams bubble from under;
Crags fall from mountain-crest.
The heights become deep vale;
Deep vates turn into height.
Men of this time bewail;
What to do with such plight?

Huang Fu presides over the state;
Fan the interior,
Jia Bo is magistrates;
Zhong Yong is minister.

Zou records worthy deeds;
Of stable Qui takes care.
Yu is captain of steeds;
All flatter Lady Bao the fair.

Oh, this Huang Fu would say
He's done all by decree.
But why drive me away
Without consulting me?
Why move my house along
And devastate my land?
Has he done nothing wrong?
The law is in his hand.

Huang Fu says he is wise
And builds the capital.
He chooses men we despise,
Corrupt and greedy all.
No men of worthy deeds
Are left to guard the crown;
Those who have cars and steeds
Are removed to his town.

I work hard all day long;
Of my toil I'm not proud.
I have done nothing wrong;
Against me stander's loud.
Distress of any kind
Does not come from on high.
Good words or bad behind
Would raise a hue and cry.

My homeland's far away;
I feel so sad and drear.
Other people are gay;
Alone I am grieved here.
When all people are free,
Why can't I take my ease?
I dread Heaven's decree;
I can't as my friends do what I please.

十月里日月之交，初一这天是辛卯。

天上现日食，多么可怕的预兆。

那月亮幽微，这太阳也幽微。

今天的老百姓，太悲哀了。

日月宣告灾难，不再走在正常轨道上。

四国不行善政，不再使用良贤。

那月食出现，还算是正常。

这日食出现，怕是要遭殃。

闪电光芒刺眼，久久不能安宁。

大江大河都泛滥，山顶突然崩塌。

原本的高崖变成深谷，昔日的深谷隆起成山岭。

哀叹当今人世，为什么罪恶从不受到惩罚？

皇父做卿士，番氏任司徒。

家伯管王家内外事务，仲允做膳夫。

聚子充内史，蹶管马匹，楀为人师。

他们和那漂亮女人都正是炙手可热。

唉这皇父啊，为什么做事不按点？

为什么叫我去干活，都不问我一声？

拆我屋墙，毁我田园，积水纵横，水草疯长。

还说自己干的不是坏事，按礼法就该这样。

皇父啊你真是太圣明，在向邑建造都城。

选择亲信做三卿，他们确实家底厚。

你不愿留下一个老成之人，守护我们的君王。

选择有车马的富豪，一起迁往你择定的向邑。

我为公事竭心尽力，原不敢说自己的辛劳。

我没有做错过任何事，却招来谗言不依不饶。

老百姓所受的苦，并不是从天而降。

当面谈笑背后憎，纷扰来自好事之人。

愁思悠悠，攒成大的心疾。

世人悠闲自得，只有我被忧愁困扰。

世人无不过得安逸，唯有我不敢片刻轻松。

天命不走寻常路，我不敢像朋友那样安逸。

这是一首政治讽刺诗。人家说天下大事肉食者谋，但作者知道"肉食者鄙"，他将那些公卿的名字一一列举，对于皇父更是有批评有讽嘲。他看清国家日渐衰落的症结，但人微言轻，甚至自身难保。可他还是不能明哲保身，忧国忧民，显示出"知其不可为而为之"的悲壮情怀，开屈原"伏清白以死直"精神之先河。

①朔月：即月朔，初一。②职竞由人：职，只。竞，纷争。这句意为"只是纷争来自好事之人"。③彻：遵循常道。

哀哉不能言，匪舌是出，维躬是瘁。哿矣能言，巧言如流，俾躬处休！

维曰于仕，孔棘且殆。云不可使，得罪于天子；亦云可使，怨及朋友。

谓尔迁于王都。曰予未有室家。鼠思泣血，无言不疾。昔尔出居，谁从作尔室？

节南山之什·雨无正

浩浩昊天，不骏其德。降丧饥馑，斩伐四国。旻天疾威，弗虑弗图。舍彼有罪，既伏其辜。若此无罪，沦胥以铺。

周宗既灭，靡所止戾。正大夫离居，莫知我勚。三事大夫，莫肯夙夜。邦君诸侯，莫肯朝夕。庶曰式臧，覆出为恶。

如何昊天，辟言不信。如彼行迈，则靡所臻。凡百君子，各敬尔身。胡不相畏，不畏于天？

戎成不退，饥成不遂。曾我暬御，憯憯日瘁。凡百君子，莫肯用讯。听言则答，谮言则退。

Untimely Rain

The heaven high,
Not kind for long,
Spreads far and nigh
Famine on throng.
Heaven unfair,
You have no care.
Nor have you thought.
Sinners are freed;
Those who sin not,
Why should, they bleed?

Where can I go after the fall
Of Zhou's capital?
Ministers gone,
None knows my toil
Nor serves the throne
But all recoil.
Of the lords none
At court appear.
No good is done
But evil here.

Why isn't just word
Believed when heard?
Travelers know
Nowhere to go.
O lords, be good
And show manhood!
Don't you revere
Heaven you fear?

After the war
Famine's not o'er.
I, a mere groom,
Am full of gloom,
Among lords who
Will speak the true?
They like good word;
Bad one's not heard.

Alas! What's true
Cannot be said,
Or woe on you,
Your tongue and head.
If you speak well
Like stream ne'er dry,
You will excel
And soon rise high.

It's hard to be
An officer.
The wrongs you see
Make you incur
Displeasure great
Of Heaven's Son,
Or in the state
Friendsyou have none.

Go back to capital!
You say your home's not there.
My bitter tears would fall

To say what you can't bear:
"When you left, who
Built house for you? "

苍天浩浩，不常降恩德。

它常降下丧乱和饥馑，席卷四方，没有人可以
逃脱。

老天肆虐，到底是想什么图什么？

放过那些有罪的人，隐匿他们的罪行。

像这些无罪的人，却让他们沦陷于痛苦之中。

周朝宗亲既然已经灭亡，没有地方可以栖身。

正大夫这六卿之长也得流亡，有谁知道我在
奔忙？

三公们地位显赫，谁肯没日没夜地操持国事？

邦君与诸侯，也不肯早晚将天子放心上。

都盼明天会更好，可是恶层出不穷。

苍天你为何这般？你听不见那法度之言！

好比远行之人，不管自己的终点。

各位君子，只管明哲保身。

互相之间毫无敬畏，更不用说敬畏老天。

战火难以消弭，饥馑已成定局。

只有我这左右之臣，成天担忧日渐憔悴。

各位君子，不肯进谏。

君王只理睬好听的，逆耳之言就叫退。

哀哉很多话不能说，不是舌头有毛病，是怕身体要遭罪。

赞啊那些巧舌如簧之辈，说瞎话真如行云流水，难怪身心都安逸。

都说做官这件事，非常艰难且危险。

动不动就说行不得，必然将天子冒犯。

昧着良心说干得好，又会让朋友们埋怨。

劝你迁回王都，你说那里没有家。

我忧愤辗转直到泣血，没有一句话不痛心疾首。

从前你逃离京都，是谁帮你修建宫殿？

　　周幽王身边的臣吏，经历了流离丧乱之后，虽然对国家心灰意冷，但仍然希望能够以一己之力回天。然而，忠言逆耳，听者昏庸，无动于衷，他也只能暗自悲伤。

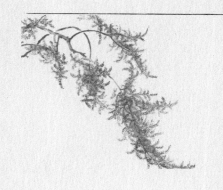

是用不溃于成。

国虽靡止，或圣或否。民虽靡膴，或哲或谋，或肃或艾。如彼泉流，无沦胥以败。

不敢暴虎，不敢冯河。人知其一，莫知其他。战战兢兢，如临深渊，如履薄冰。

节南山之什 · 小旻

旻天疾威，敷于下土。谋犹回遹，何日斯沮？谋臧不从，不臧覆用。我视谋犹，亦孔之邛。

潝潝訿訿，亦孔之哀。谋之其臧，则具是违。谋之不臧，则具是依。我视谋犹，伊于胡底。

我龟既厌，不我告犹。谋夫孔多，是用不集。发言盈庭，谁敢执其咎？如匪行迈谋，是用不得于道。

哀哉为犹，匪先民是程，匪大犹是经。维迩言是听，维迩言是争。如彼筑室于道谋，

Counselors

The Heaven's ire.
On earth descends.
The counsels dire
Go without ends.
They follow one
Not good but bad.
The good not done,
I feel so sad.

Controversy
Is to be rued.
They disagree
On what is good.
On what is bad
They will depend.
I feel not glad;
How will this end?

The tortoise bored,
Nothing's foretold.
Men on the board
No right uphold.
The more they say;
The less they do.
They won't start on their way.
How can we ask them to?

Alas! Formers of plan
Won't follow those of yore.
No principles they can
Formulate as before.
They follow counselors
Who can nothing good yield.
They ask the wayfarers
About houses to build.

Though bounded is our state,
Our men may be wise or not.
Our numbers are not great;
Some know to plan and plot;
Others are able to think
Like stream from spring will flow.
Together they will sink
In common weal and woe.

Don't fight a tiger with bare hand,
Nor cross without a boat the stream.
You may know one thing in your land,
But not another as you deem.
Be careful as if you did stand
On the brink of the gulf of vice
Or tread upon thin ice!

*

老天何其暴虐，灾难撒播人间。

应对的主意皆邪门，何时才能了结？

好的主意你不听，坏点子你倒是用。

我看你现在那些政策，都有很大的弊端。

潝潝附和，訿訿毁谤，好不热闹，令人哀伤。

好主意，全放一旁。

坏主意，言听计从。

我看你昏招这么多，要把国家变啥样。

灵龟想来也已经厌烦，不肯告诉我天机。

谋士那么多，全部不能成事。

你听人声鼎沸，装满整个大厅，谁敢承担责任？

就像去问不走远路的人，得到的答案无法用在路上。

可叹你们的谋略，不去效法先民，不去走那大道。

只爱听那没有远见的话，只爱争那眼皮子底下的事。

就像盖房子偏去问路上的人，肯定无法完成。

国家虽然不算大，也有圣人和普通人。

老百姓虽然不算多，也有智者善谋者。

有谨慎的人，有善于治理的人。

朝政就像流动的泉水，不要相继败落。

不能徒手搏虎，不敢徒步过河。

众人只知其一，不知道的还有很多。

你只能是战战兢兢，像是面临深渊，像是踩在薄冰上。

　　这一首诗也是讽刺周幽王的。幽王昏庸无道，任用佞臣，无法判断谋略的好坏。看上去是不够勇敢，其实是内部已经腐朽。诗人知道得太多太多，心里难免战战兢兢。

或以其酒，不以其浆。鞙鞙[xuàn]佩璲，不以其长。维天有汉，监亦有光。跂彼织女，

终日七襄。

虽则七襄，不成报章。睆彼牵牛，不以服箱。东有启明，西有长庚。有捄天毕，

载施之行。

维南有箕，不可以簸扬。维北有斗，不可以挹酒浆。维南有箕，载翕其舌。

维北有斗，西柄之揭。

谷风之什·大东

有饛簋飧，有捄棘匕。周道如砥，其直如矢。君子所履，小人所视。睠言顾之，潸焉出涕。

小东大东，杼柚其空。纠纠葛屦，可以履霜。佻佻公子，行彼周行。既往既来，使我心疚。

有冽氿泉，无浸获薪。契契寤叹，哀我惮人。薪是获薪，尚可载也。哀我惮人，亦可息也。

东人之子，职劳不来。西人之子，粲粲衣服。舟人之子，熊罴是裘。私人之子，百僚是试。

East and West

The tripod's full of food;
They eat with spoons of wood.
The road's smooth like whetstone
For lords to go alone.
Like arrow it is straight,
On which no people circulate.
Recalling bygone years,
In streams run down my tears.

In east states, large and small,
The looms are empty all.
In summer shoes we go
On winter frost or snow.
Even the noble sons
Walk on foot like poor ones.
Seeing them come and go,
My heart is full of woe.

Cold water passing by,
Do not soak our firewood!
Woeful we wake and sigh
For scanty livelihood.
If our firewood is dry,
We may carry it west.
If wet, we can but sigh.
O when may we have rest?

We toilers of the East.
Are not paid as those of the West;
The western nobles at least
Are all splendidly drest.

The rich and noble sons
Don't care about their furs,
But as slaves the poor ones
Serve all the officers.

If we present them wine,
They do not think it fine.
If we present them jade,
They don't think it well-made.
The Silver River bright
Looks down on us in light.
The Weaving Stars are three;
All day long they are free.

Though all day long they move,
They weave nothing above.
Bright is the Cowherd Star,
But it won't draw our car.
Morning Star in the east,
Eight Net Stars catch no beast,
Evening Star in the west,
What use though they don't rest?

In south the Winnowing Fan
Cannot sift grain for man.
In north the Dipper fine
Cannot ladle good wine.
The Sieve shines in the south,
Idly showing its mouth.
In the north shines the Plough
With handle like a bow.

满满的食器，弯弯的勺。

大路像是被谁磨平，笔直如箭矢。

君子们行其上，小人物旁边望。

回头看了又看，不由得涕泪潸然。

东方那远近城邦，织布机上已被掠光。

葛藤缠做鞋子，可以踩踏水霜。

那些轻佻的公子，走在大道上。

走来又走去，让我看了心伤。

那冷冽的侧出泉，不要浸泡我砍下的柴薪。

我睡不着声声长叹，请哀怜我这辛苦的人。

若是把荻薪当柴烧，尚且可以载回去。

若哀怜我这辛劳的人，也许还可以休息。

东边人的子弟，辛苦无人安慰。

西边人的子弟，总是衣着华丽。

船户之家的子弟，熊皮袍子穿上身。

家奴的子弟，将来也能当官吏。

那美酒之好，不在干浆。

玉佩之美，不在其长。

天上有河汉，亮闪闪如镜子一样。

织女星双脚站立，一天转换七个地方。

虽然换了七个地方，也不能织成布匹。

牵牛星耀眼明亮，但是拉不动车辆。

东边有启明星，西边有长庚星。

还有弯弯的天毕星，一路蔓延放光。

南边簸箕星，不可以拿来筛糠。

北边有北斗星，不可以舀酒浆。

南边有簸箕星，吐着它的舌头。

北边有北斗星，斗柄指向西方。

这是一首针砭时弊的长诗。东方诸侯国的人辛苦劳动，成果却被西人和周朝贵族洗劫一空。作者看着他们趾高气扬走在大路上，锦衣玉食，心中非常不甘。地上的事无足观，只能把目光转向天空，但一肚子没好气去看天；只觉得天上的人像自己一样辛劳。全诗运用对比和暗喻的修辞手法，由人间转入星空，展现了东方诸侯国民众遭受沉重压榨的困苦境遇和作者忧愤抗争的情怀。

礼仪既备，钟鼓既戒。孝孙徂位，工祝致告。神具醉止，皇尸载起。

鼓钟送尸，神保聿归。诸宰君妇，废彻不迟。诸父兄弟，备言燕私。

乐具入奏，以绥后禄。尔肴既将，莫怨具庆。既醉既饱，小大稽首。

神嗜饮食，使君寿考。孔惠孔时，维其尽之。子子孙孙，勿替引之。

谷风之什·楚茨

楚楚者茨，言抽其棘。自昔何为，我艺黍稷。我黍与与，我稷翼翼。

我仓既盈，我庾维亿。以为酒食，以享以祀。以妥以侑，以介景福。

济济跄跄，絜尔牛羊，以往烝尝。或剥或亨，或肆或将。

祝祭于祊，祀事孔明。先祖是皇，神保是飨。孝孙有庆，报以介福，万寿无疆。

执爨踖踖，为俎孔硕。或燔或炙，君妇莫莫。为豆孔庶，为宾为客。

献酬交错，礼仪卒度，笑语卒获。神保是格，报以介福，万寿攸酢。

我孔熯矣，式礼莫愆。工祝致告，徂赉孝孙。苾芬孝祀，神嗜饮食。

卜尔百福，如几如式。既齐既稷，既匡既敕。永锡尔极，时万时亿。

Winter Sacrifice

O let us clear away
All the overgrown thorns!
Just as in olden days
We plant millet and corns.
Our millet overgrows
And our barns stand in rows;

Our sorghum overgrows
And our stacks stand in rows.
We prepare wine and meat
For temple sacrifice;
We urge spirits to eat
And invoke blessings thrice.

We clean the oxen nice
And offer them in heap
For winter sacrifice.
We flay and broil the sheep
And cut and carve the meat.

The priest's at the temple gate
Till service is complete.
Then come our fathers great.
They enjoy food and wine
And to their grandson say,
"Receive blessings divine,
Live long and be e'er gay! "

The cooks work with great skill
And prepare all the trays.
They roast or broil at will;

Women help them always.
Smaller dishes abound
For the guests left and right.

They raise cups and drink round
According to the rite.
They laugh and talk at will
When witches come and say,
"Receive more blessings still;
Live long with glee for aye! "

With respect we fulfil
The due rites one by one.
The priests announce the will
Of spirits to grandson:
"Fragrant's the sacrifice;
They enjoy meat and wine.

They confer blessings thrice
On you for rites divine.
You have done what is due
Correctly with good care.
Favors conferred on you
Will be found everywhere. "

The ceremonies done,
Drums beaten and bells rung,
In his place the grandson,
The priest then gives his tongue:
"The spirits drunken well,
The dead ready to go. "

Let's beat drum and ring bell
For them to go below!
Cooks and women, come here.
Remove trays without delay.
Uncles and cousins dear,
At private feast let's stay.

Music played in the hall,
We eat when spirits go.
Enjoying dishes, all
Forget their former woe.
They drink their fill and eat,
Bowing the head, old and young.

"The spirits love your meat
And will make you live long.
Your rites are duly done;
You are pious and nice.
Let nor son nor grandson
Forget the sacrifice! "

蒺藜纵横，我除荆棘。

当年何为？我种黍稷。

我黍茂盛，我稷齐整。

我的仓廪丰盈，我的晒谷场数不清。

拿来烹做酒食，请祖宗们享用。

请他们安享，赐我们宏大幸福。

子孙密密匝匝，依然奔走有序。

洗净你的牛羊，拿去做秋冬祭享。

有人在剥皮有人在烹煮，有人布置有人双手捧上。

司仪在庙门里祭神，全程多么完备。

先祖到来，神灵将酒肉品尝。

孝孙有福，请赐予更大的幸福，万寿无疆。

厨子谨慎，食器硕大。

又烧又烤，主妇沉着。

碗中餐何其丰富，呈给那些宾客。

觥筹交错，礼仪合度，笑语尽兴。

神灵已经来到，赐予大福，赐万寿为回报。

我是多么恭谨，每个礼节都周到。

司仪转达祖先的回复：

即将赏赐这些孝孙。祭品美味，为神所爱。
赐你百样福分，满足你的期许又不逾矩。你们的
祭祀恭而快，端正又严肃。赐你福气的无极，
万万亿亿。

礼仪已经完备，钟鼓也已经齐备。

孝孙走回原位，司仪将神的声音向大家转告：
"神灵都已喝醉。"

神尸起身。

钟鼓送之，祖宗踏上归程。

厨子和主妇，快快撤去祭品。

诸位父老兄弟，开始自己的宴饮。

乐队开始演奏，继续安享幸福。

你们的菜肴多美味，无人抱怨，全都在欢庆。

吃饱喝醉，大人小孩齐齐跪拜。

神爱吃这样的酒食，让大家长寿延年。

多么好又多么合乎时辰，你们尽到自己的心意。

愿子子孙孙，将这祭礼，继承下去。

　　这是周王祭祖祭神的乐歌。一场宏大的祭祀，从准备
祭品，到请神，再到送神，最后才是自己私下的宴饮，详
细展现了周代祭祀的仪制风貌。但《毛诗序》认为，它是
对幽王的讽刺，讽刺幽王"政烦赋重，田莱多荒，饥馑降
丧，民卒流亡，祭祀不飨，故君子思古焉"。

甫田之什·頍弁

有頍（kuǐ）者弁，实维伊何？尔酒既旨，尔殽既嘉。岂伊异人？兄弟匪他。
茑与女萝，施于松柏。未见君子，忧心奕奕；既见君子，庶几说怿。

有頍者弁，实维何期？尔酒既旨，尔殽既时。岂伊异人？兄弟具来。
茑与女萝，施于松上。未见君子，忧心怲怲；既见君子，庶几有臧。

有頍者弁，实维在首。尔酒既旨，尔殽既阜。岂伊异人？兄弟甥舅。
如彼雨雪，先集维霰。死丧无日，无几相见。乐酒今夕，君子维宴。

The Royal Banquet

Who are those lords so fine
In leather cap or hood,
Coming to drink your wine
And eat your viands good?
Can they be others?
They are your brothers.

They are like mistletoe
That o'er cypress does grow.
When they see you not, how
Can their hearts not be sad?
When they do see you now,
They are happy and glad.

Who are those lords so fine
In deer skin cap or hood,
Coming to drink your wine
And eat your seasonable food?
Can they be others?
They are your brothers.

They are like mistletoe
That o'er the pine does grow.
When they see you not, how
Can their hearts not feel sad?
When they do see you now,
They feel all right and glad.

Who are those lords so fine
With leather cap on head,
Coming to drink your wine,
With food the table spread?
O how can they be others?
They are our cousins and brothers.

We are like snow or rain;
Nothing will long remain.
Death may come any day;
We can enjoy tonight at least.
Drink and rejoice as you may;
Let us enjoy the feast!

你戴着尖顶皮帽，如此郑重为何？

你的酒那么美味，你的菜肴很不错。

哪有什么外人，大家都是兄弟。

茑草与女萝，缠绕着松柏。

没有见到君子您，我心里担忧得直打鼓。

直到看见君子您，才算心里始欢畅。

你戴着尖顶皮帽，如此郑重为何？

你的酒那么美味，你的菜肴刚刚出锅。

哪有什么外人？大家都是兄弟。

茑草与女萝，缠绕着松柏。

没有见到君子您，我心里担忧得直犯嘀咕。

直到看见君子您，才算心情变美好。

你戴着尖顶皮帽，好好地戴在头上。

你的酒那么美味，你的菜肴也很丰富。

哪有什么外人，都是兄弟甥舅。

人生如同雨雪，先是雪珠聚集。

死丧没有日期，还有几回聚集。

今天且进美酒，感谢君子的宴请。

　　此诗借赴宴者的视角，描述了贵族间彼
此依附的关系，在表现赴宴者阿谀奉承的同
时，也展现了贵族醉生梦死的生活，流露出
暗淡低沉、悲观失望的情绪。主人衣着郑重，
请的都是兄弟甥舅。作者将自己比喻成茑萝，
将主人比喻成松柏，未见到对方，内心不安，
见到对方，才高兴起来。

　　虽然有美酒佳肴，宾主尽欢，但世上事
总是乐极生悲。欢快的气氛，让人想起丧失
的悲伤；诗歌结尾忽然转向幽暗，寓意世间
欢乐，都建立于死亡底色之上。

甫田之什·车舝

间关车之舝^{xiá}兮，思娈季女逝兮。匪饥匪渴，德音来括。虽无好友？式燕且喜。

依彼平林，有集维鷮。辰彼硕女，令德来教。式燕且誉，好尔无射。^①

虽无旨酒？式饮庶几。虽无嘉殽？式食庶几。虽无德与女？式歌且舞？

陟彼高冈，析其柞薪。析其柞薪，其叶湑兮。鲜我觏尔，我心写兮。

高山仰止，景行行止。四牡骓骓，六辔如琴。觏尔新婚，以慰我心。

On the Way to the Bride's House

Having prepared my creaking cart,
I go to fetch my bride.
Nor hungry nor thirsty at heart,
I'll take her as good guide,
Nor good friends come nor priest;
We'll rejoice in our feast.

In the plain there's dense wood
And pheasants with long tail.
I love my young bride good;
She'll help me without fail.
I'll praise her when we feast,
Never tired in the least.

Though we have no good wine,
We'll drink, avoiding waste.
Though our viands are not fine,
We may give them a taste.
Though no good to you can I bring,
Still we may dance and sing.

I climb the mountain green
To split oak for firewood.
Amid leaves lush and green
I split oak for firewood.
Seeing my matchless bride,
I will be satisfied.

You're good like mountains high;
Like the road you go long.
My four steeds run and hie;
Six reins like lute-strings weave a song.
When I'm wed to my bride,
How my heart will be satisfied!

呦
呦
鹿
鸣
＊
美
得
窒
息
的
诗
经

高
山
仰
止

车轴转动了，美丽的少女要出嫁了。

倒不是我如饥似渴，是这姑娘拥有百样美德。

婚宴虽然没有好朋友，随便喝酒也很快乐。

平林茂密，野鸡站立。

善良健壮的姑娘，她的德行多美好。

且饮酒作乐，我对你的爱，永不会疲倦。

虽然没有美酒，也请你喝几杯。

虽然没有佳肴，也请你尝几口。

虽然没有美德可以感染你，不妨在当下且歌且舞。

登上那高冈，砍下柞树枝条当柴烧。

砍下柞树枝条当柴烧，它的叶子茂密。

难得见到你，我心中无限欢喜。

高山唯有仰望，大道且去行走。

四匹马啪嗒啪嗒走，六根缰绳如琴弦。

新婚之时看到你，我心中无限欢喜。

这是一首歌咏新婚的乐章，堪称一曲美好爱情的颂歌。男子娶到心爱的姑娘，快乐得颠三倒四；明明急不可耐，还要声称是喜欢人家的美德。无所谓来的是不是好友，这样的大好日子，不管谁来喝喜酒，都是受欢迎的嘉客。新郎驾着彩车迎娶新娘，憧憬着未来的美好生活，洋溢着欢快的情绪。

①射：厌烦。

甫田之什·青蝇

营营青蝇，止于樊。岂弟君子，无信谗言。

营营青蝇，止于棘。谗人罔极，交乱四国。

营营青蝇，止于榛。谗人罔极，构我二人。

Blue Flies

Hear the buzzing blue flies;
On the fence they alight.
Lord, don't believe their lies;
Friend, don't take wrong for right.

Hear blue flies buzzing, friend;
They light on jujube trees.

The slander without end
Spreads in the state disease.

Hear blue flies buzzing, friend;
They light on hazel tree.
The slander without end
Sets you at odds with me.

苍蝇飞来飞去，落在篱笆上。

温和的君子，不信谗言。

苍蝇飞来飞去，落在荆棘上。

满嘴谗言的人太没品德，一心搅乱这世界。

苍蝇飞来飞去，落在榛树上。

满嘴谗言的人太没品德，离间你我的交情。

　　这是一首著名的谴责诗，讽刺统治者听信谗言，斥责谗人害人祸国。性情温和，平易近人的人，不急躁，不主观，通常不会相信谣言。谣言能危害到的，是急躁且没有安全感的人。

屡舞傞傞。既醉而出，并受其福。醉而不出，是谓伐德。饮酒孔嘉，维其令仪。

凡此饮酒，或醉或否。既立之监，或佐之史。彼醉不臧，不醉反耻。式勿从谓，

无俾大怠。匪言勿言，匪由勿语。由醉之言，俾出童羖。三爵不识，矧敢多又。

甫田之什·宾之初筵

宾之初筵，左右秩秩。笾豆有楚，殽核维旅。酒既和旨，饮酒孔偕。钟鼓既设，

举酬逸逸。大侯既抗，弓矢斯张。射夫既同，献尔发功。发彼有的，以祈尔爵。

籥舞笙鼓，乐既和奏。烝衎烈祖，以洽百礼。百礼既至，有壬有林。锡尔纯嘏，

子孙其湛。其湛曰乐，各奏尔能。宾载手仇，室人入又。酌彼康爵，以奏尔时。①②

宾之初筵，温温其恭。其未醉止，威仪反反。曰既醉止，威仪幡幡。舍其坐迁，

屡舞仙仙。其未醉止，威仪抑抑。曰既醉止，威仪怭怭。是曰既醉，不知其秩。

宾既醉止，载号载呶。乱我笾豆，屡舞傲傲。是曰既醉，不知其邮。侧弁之俄，

Revelry

The guests come with delight
And take place left and right.
In rows arranged the dishes,
Displayed viands and fishes.
The wine is mild and good;
Guests drink and eat the food.
Bells and drums in their place,
They raise their cups with grace.

The target set on foot,
With bows for them to shoot,
The archers stand in row,
Ready their skill to show.
If the target is hit,
You'll drink a cup for it.

They dance to music sweet
Of flute and to drumbeat.
Rites are performed to please
Our ancestors with ease.
The offerings on hand
Are so full and so grand.
You will be richly blessed,
Sons, grandsons and the rest.

Happy is every man.
Let each do what he can.
Each guest shoots with his bow;
The host joins in the row.
Let's fill an empty cup.
When one hits, all cheer up.

When guests begin to feast,
They are gentle at least.
When they've not drunk too much,
They would observe the rite;
When they have drunk too much,
Their deportment is light.
They leave their seats and go
Capering to and fro.

When they've not drunk too much,
They are in a good mood;
When they have drunk too much,
They're indecent and rude.
When they are deeply drunk,
They know not where they're sunk.

When they've drunk their cups dry,
They shout out, brawl and cry.
They put plates upside down;
They dance like funny clown.
When they have drunk wine strong,
They know not right from wrong.
With their cups on one side,
They dance and slip and slide.

If drunk they went away,
The host would happy stay.
But drunk they will not go;
The host is full of woe.
We may drink with delight.
If we observe the rite.

Whenever people drink,
In drunkenness some sink.
Appoint an inspector
And keep a register.
But drunkards feel no shame;
On others they'll lay blame.
Don't drink any more toast,
Or they will wrong the host.

Do not speak if you could;
Say only what you should.
Don't say like drunkard born.
You're a ram without horn.
With three cups you've lost head;
With more you'd be drunk dead.

宾客刚刚落座，左右排列有序。

餐具摆放齐整，菜肴果品皆备。

美酒原本醇正，那就快乐地喝起。

钟鼓放置在一旁，举杯敬酒不停歇。

箭靶已经竖起，弓矢也已经张开。

射箭者已经到齐，快表现你的功力。

若是正中靶心，就要罚你的对手喝一杯。

执籥而舞，敲起笙鼓，众乐合奏。

承欢列祖，这合乎各种礼法。

百礼既至，何其盛大。

赐你大福，子孙和乐。

每个人都欢天喜地，各显其能。

宾客们各取对手，主人再次加入。

给大酒杯斟满酒，祝贺你这位射中者。

宾客刚刚落座，个个温良恭俭。

还没醉倒的时候，看似威仪赫赫。

等到他们喝醉，威仪丢到一边。

离席跑到别处，手舞足蹈要上天。

他们没醉的时候，保持着威仪体面。

等到他们喝醉，满脸轻薄笑意。

所以说一旦喝醉，哪还管什么秩序。

宾客彻底喝醉，一边号一边闹。

弄乱人家的杯盘，屡屡跳起舞蹈。

所以说一旦喝醉，哪还管什么对不对。

把皮帽子歪戴在头顶，蹦跳着舞个没完。

既然喝醉就该出去，大家都享你的福气。

喝多了还赖在这儿，简直没有德行。

喝酒本是好事，但也要遵守礼仪。

所以关于饮酒，不管是醉或没醉，都要设个酒监，还要弄个酒史将所有行为记录在案。

喝醉了很不好，他们还要说没醉的很可耻。

你不要顺着醉鬼来，也不要煽风点火地让他出丑。

不该说的不要说，不该问的不要问。

喝醉的人说话哪有准，张嘴说公羊没有角。

三杯下肚人事不知，哪经得你再去挑逗。

　　这首诗通过描写宴饮的场面，讽刺了酒后失仪、失言、失德的种种醉态，提出了反对滥饮的主张。描述了人们从拘谨到喝醉的全过程，先是井然有序，然后宾客血液燃烧，手舞足蹈，帽子歪戴，任人驱逐还赖着不走。为了防止好好的饭局被这种酒鬼搅和了，只有设下酒监，还要记录在案。虽然这首诗经常被解释为讽刺贵族的，但普通人喝多了，也是一个德行。

①有壬有林：壬，大。林，多。②时：《毛传》："时，中者也。"

第四章

鹤鸣
×
九皋

CHAPTER FOUR

In the marsh the crane cries;
Her voice is heard for miles

维柞之枝，其叶蓬蓬。乐只君子，殿天子
之邦。乐只君子，万福攸同。平平左右，
亦是率从。

汎汎杨舟，绋纚维之。乐只君子，天子葵之。

乐只君子，福禄脞之。优哉游哉，亦是戾矣。

Royal Favours

Gather beans long and short
In baskets round and square.
The lords come to the court.
What suitable things there
Can be given to meet their needs?
A state cab and horses four.
What else besides the steeds?
Dragon robes they adore.

Gather cress long and short
Around the spring near by.
The lords come to the court;
I see dragon flags fly.
Flags flutter in the breeze,
Three or four horses run,
Bells ringing without cease,
The lords come one by one.

Red covers on their knees
And their buskins below,
They go with perfect ease
In what the king bestows.
They receive with delight
High favours from the king;

(四)

鹤鸣九皋

鱼藻之什 · 采菽

采菽采菽，筐之筥之。君子来朝，何锡予之？

虽无予之？路车乘马。又何予之？玄衮及黼。

觱沸槛泉，言采其芹。君子来朝，言观其旂。bi

其旂淠淠，鸾声嘒嘒。载骖载驷，君子所届。

赤芾在股，邪幅在下。彼交匪纾，天子所予。

乐只君子，天子命之。乐只君子，福禄申之。

Follow them where they go.

The boat of willow wood
Fastened by band and rope,
Of happy lords and good
The king scans the full scope.
They receive with high glee
All blessings from the king.
They're happy and carefree;
Fortune comes on the wing.

They receive with delight
Good fortune in a string.

On branches of oak-tree,
What riot lush leaves run!
The lords guard with high glee
The land of Heaven's Son.
They receive with delight
Blessings from high and low.
Attendants left and right

采豆采豆，装入方的圆的筐。

君子来朝，天子怎么赏？

赏之不多，四马拉路车。

还赏了什么？那绘着龙纹的黑白华裳。

泉水翻腾，可采芹菜。

君子来朝，天子迎到旌旗前。

看他旌旗飘动，马车铃声叮当。

众马驾车，将君子送到眼前。

红色蔽膝护住膝股，裹腿布在它下面。

不交缠也不怠慢，因是天子赏赐。

何其快乐啊君子，天子要你如此。

何其快乐啊君子，你的福禄一再堆积。

柞树枝条上，其叶蓬蓬。

何其快乐啊君子，你镇抚天子的土地。

何其快乐啊君子，所有的福分一同到来。

左右臣下都能干，和你一样唯天子是从。

杨木小舟河中漂，需要缆绳固定。

何其快乐啊君子，天子衡量你的才能。

何其快乐啊君子，福禄都将赐给你。

优哉游哉，生活得多么安定。

　　天子接见诸侯，有很多恩宠赏赐，有人
作这首诗助兴，劝诫诸侯安分守己。然而，
诸侯中亦有野心者，怕是不能"乐只君子"。
因此，天子恩赏的另一面，是无所不在的控制。
此诗总体上以赋法为主，展现了一幅周代诸
侯朝见天子时的历史画卷。

鱼藻之什·角弓

骍骍角弓，翩其反矣。兄弟昏姻，无胥远矣。尔之远矣，民胥然矣。尔之教矣，民胥效矣。

此令兄弟，绰绰有裕。不令兄弟，交相为瘉。民之无良，相怨一方。受爵不让，至于己斯亡。

老马反为驹，不顾其后。如食宜饇，yù 如酌孔取。毋教猱升木，如涂涂附。

君子有徽猷，小人与属。

雨雪瀌瀌，见晛曰消。莫肯下遗，式居娄骄。雨雪浮浮，见晛曰流。如蛮如髦，我是用忧。

Admonition

Tighten the string of the bow,
Its recoil will be swift.
If brothers alien go,
Their affection will shift.
If you alienate
Your relatives and brothers,
People will imitate
You when you deal with others.

When there is brotherhood,
Good feeling is displayed.
When brothers are not good,
Much trouble will be made.
The people have no grace,
They blame the other side;
They fight to get high place
And come to fratricide.

Old steeds think themselves good;
Of the young they don't think.
They want plenty of food
And an excess of drink.
Don't teach apes to climb trees.
Nor add mud to the wall.
If you do good with ease,
They'll follow you one and all.

Flake on flake falls the snow;
It dissolves in the sun.
Don't despise those below.
The proud will be undone.
The snow falls flake on flake;
It will melt in sunlight,
Let no barbarians make
You fall into a sad plight.

才调和好角弓，卸弦它就往里翻。

兄弟之间，千万不要疏远。

你们要是疏远，老百姓也会这样。

你们的言传身教，老百姓都会效仿。

兄弟友好相处，生活就变得舒缓。

兄弟们互不待见，坐下心病互相怨。

可惜现在人们不怎么善良，动不动就怨恨对方。

接受爵位绝不推让，关乎私利就会将仁义遗忘。

老马反当马驹使，谁管它后来怎么样。

就像吃饭吃太饱，就像喝酒太过量。

猴子上树不必教，就像泥浆粘上墙。

君子若是有正道，凡人自然跟着跑。

雨雪瀌瀌，见日气而消。

你待下人不谦和，人家见你也不客气。

雨雪浮浮，见日气而流。

大家现在都像野蛮人，想起来就难免心忧。

　　这是劝告周王不要疏远兄弟亲戚而亲近小人的诗。传统道德里，除了孝，最重要的就是悌，也就是兄弟关系。兄弟关系顺了，一切都顺了，毕竟，四海之内皆兄弟；这个关系是可以像水波一样一层层向外推的。

　　然而，帝王家族的兄弟关系往往最容易出问题，《左传》中的一篇《郑伯克段于鄢》，讲述的是郑庄公同其胞弟共叔段之间为了夺取君位而进行的一场你死我活的斗争。

　　上行下效，世风日下，呜呼哀哉。这首诗正是对身居高位者苦口婆心的劝诫。

鱼藻之什·菀柳

有菀者柳，不尚息焉。上帝甚蹈，无自昵焉。

俾予靖之，后予极焉。①

有菀者柳，不尚愒焉。上帝甚蹈，无自瘵焉。②zhài

俾予靖之，后予迈焉。

有鸟高飞，亦傅于天。彼人之心，于何其臻。

曷予靖之，居以凶矜。

The Unjust Lord

Lush is the willow tree.
Who won't rest under it?
The lord's to punish free.
Don't fall into the pit.
You lend him hand and arm,
But he will do you harm.

Lush is the willow tree.
Who won't shelter'neath it?
The lord's to punish free;

His ire bursts in a fit.
You lend him arm and hand;
He'll ban you from the land.

The bird flies as it can
Even up to the sky.
The heart of such a man
Will go up far and high.
Whate'er for him you do,
He's free to punish you.

你看那柳树已枯萎，就不要靠上去休息了。
你看君王不靠谱，就不要去亲近他。
当初让我管国事，后来又将我惩罚。

你看那柳树已枯萎，就不要靠上去休息了。
你看君主不靠谱，就不要自找麻烦了。
当初让我管国事，后来又将我放逐。

鸟儿不妨高飞，到那天之高处。
那个人的心，能狠到何等地步。
为何叫我管国事，又将我推到这凶险之地。

　　这是一首揭露王者喜怒无常，残暴虐待
诸侯的诗。向来君心难测，将你委以重任的
是他，担心你功高盖主而置于死地的也是他。
就像宋高宗对待岳飞一样，曾经有过亲密信
任的时刻，然而风云变幻，他就成了罪臣。
这首诗，也可作岳飞的心声。

①极：通"殛"，惩罚，放逐。②瘵：病。

鱼藻之什·黍苗

芃芃黍苗，阴雨膏之。悠悠南行，召伯劳之。

我任我辇，我车我牛。我行既集，盖云归哉。

我徒我御，我师我旅。我行既集，盖云归处。

肃肃谢功，召伯营之。烈烈征师，召伯成之。

原隰既平，泉流既清。召伯有成，王心则宁。

Young millet grows tall and strong,
Fattened by genial rain.
Our southward journey's long;
The Lord of Shao cheers the train.

Our carts go one by one;
Our oxen follow the track.
Our construction is done,
So we are going back.

We go on foot or run;
Our host goes in a throng.

Our construction is done,
So we are going along.

The town of Xie stands strong,
Built by our lord with might and main.
Our expedition's long.
And our lord leads the train.

Lowland becomes a plain;
Streams are cleared east and west.
Our lord leads the campaign;
The king's heart is at rest.

黍苗繁茂，雨水滋润。
我们悠悠南行，有召伯犒劳。

有的拉车有的扛物，有的推车有的牵牛。
我们的任务已经完成，就要回归故里。

有的徒步有的驾驶，被编成各和队伍。
我们的任务已经完成，就要回归故里。

修筑谢城，是庄严的工程，幸有召伯来经营。
威武的出征之师，是召伯建成。

高原湿地已经平整，泉水已经变清。
召伯有这么大的成就，王的心终可以安宁。

　　周宣王让召伯（即召穆公）征集劳力营
治谢邑。工程结束后，服劳役者感到与有荣焉，
对召伯由衷地赞美。此诗是参与工程建设的
徒役在完成任务于归途之中的歌唱。

鱼藻之什·瓠叶

幡幡瓠叶，采之亨之。君子有酒，酌言尝之。

有兔斯首，炮之燔之。君子有酒，酌言献之。

有兔斯首，燔之炙之。君子有酒，酌言酢之。

有兔斯首，燔之炮之。君子有酒，酌言酬之。

Frugal Hospitality

The gourd's waving leaves are fine,
Taken and boiled in haste.
Our good friend has sweet wine;
He pours it out for a taste.

The rabbit's meat is fine
When baked or roasted up.
Our good friend has sweet wine;
He presents us a cup.

The rabbit's meat is fine
When broiled or roasted up,
Our good friend has sweet wine;
We present him a cup.

The rabbit's meat is fine
When baked or roasted up.
Our good friend has sweet wine;
We fill each other's cup.

瓠叶翻飞，采之烹之。君子有酒，斟满请你品尝。

白色的兔头，裹泥或者拔毛烧烤，君子有酒，斟满呈献给你。

白色的兔头，拔掉毛做成烤串，君子有酒，客人回敬主人。

白色的兔头，拔掉毛或裹上泥烤，君子有酒，大家殷勤互劝。

《诗序》说这首诗是"大夫刺幽王也"，因为"弃礼而不行"，所以"思古之人，不以微薄废礼焉"。但阅读这首诗，感觉不出这种崇高的意味，只觉得古人吃兔头的历史竟然这么悠久，吃法也很诱人。

文王之什·思齐

思齐大任，文王之母，思媚周姜，京室之妇。大姒嗣徽音，则百斯男。

惠于宗公，神罔时怨，神罔时恫。刑于寡妻，至于兄弟，以御于家邦。

雍雍在宫，肃肃在庙。不显亦临，无射亦保。①

肆戎疾不殄，②烈假不瑕。不闻亦式，不谏亦入。

肆成人有德，小子有造。古之人无斁，③誉髦斯士。

King Wen's Reign

Reverent Lady Ren
Was mother of King Wen.
She loved grandmother dear,
A good wife without peer.
Si inherited her fame;
From her a hundred sons came.

Good done to fathers dead,
Nowhere complaint was spread,
They reposed as they could.
King Wen set example good
To his dear wife and brothers,
His countrymen and others.

At home benevolent,
In temple reverent,
He had gods e'er in view;
No wrong would he e'er do.

All evils rectified,
No ill done far and wide.
Untaught, he knew the right;
Advised, he saw the light.

The grown-up became good;
E'en the young showed manhood.
All talents sang in praise
Of King Wen's olden days.

　　庄重的大任，是文王的母亲。

　　美好的周姜，周王室的主妇。

　　文王之妃大姒，继承这美好的名声，必然有无数子嗣。

　　顺从先祖遗训，鬼神就无所怨，鬼神就无所痛。

　　给正妻做出示范；还能影响到兄弟，及至于家邦。

　　在宫中他舒缓温和，在宗庙他庄严持重。

　　在天光下他会自我审查，在幽隐处他依旧慎独。

　　如今西戎不为患，病魔亦不害人民。

　　纵然之前无所闻，他仍然在规则内。

　　纵然没有劝谏者，他仍然在善之中。

　　所以他治下的成人都品德高尚，年轻人都有所作为。

　　古人精神不会被破坏，俊杰之士都会得到赞赏。

这是歌颂周文王善于修身、齐家、治国的诗篇。君主不但是一国的统治者，也是一国的精神领袖。他需要全方位做出榜样，首先影响身边人，比如妻子和兄弟，然后影响整个国家。此诗反映出传统道德在周文王身上的完美体现。

①射：通"斁"。②烈假：害人的疾病。③斁：厌弃，破坏。

帝谓文王：无然畔援，无然歆羡，诞先登于岸。密人不恭，敢距大邦，侵阮徂共。

王赫斯怒，爰整其旅，以按徂旅。以笃于周祜，以对于天下。

依其在京，侵自阮疆。陟我高冈，无矢我陵。我陵我阿，无饮我泉，我泉我池。

度其鲜原，居岐之阳，在渭之将。万邦之方，下民之王。

帝谓文王：予怀明德，不大声以色，不长夏以革。不识不知，顺帝之则。帝

谓文王：询尔仇方，同尔弟兄。以尔钩援，与尔临冲，以伐崇墉。

临冲闲闲，崇墉言言。执讯连连，攸馘^{guó}③安安。是类是祃^{mà}，是致是附，四方以无侮。

临冲茀茀，崇墉仡仡。是伐是肆，是绝是忽。四方以无拂。

文王之什·皇矣

皇矣上帝，临下有赫。监观四方，求民之莫。维此二国，其政不获。维彼四国，

爰究爰度。上帝耆之^①，憎其式廓^②。乃眷西顾，此维与宅。

作之屏之，其菑其翳。修之平之，其灌其栵。启之辟之，其柽其椐。攘之剔之，

其檿其柘。帝迁明德，串夷载路。天立厥配，受命既固。

帝省其山，柞棫斯拔，松柏斯兑。帝作邦作对，自大伯王季。维此王季，因心则友。

则友其兄，则笃其庆，载锡之光。受禄无丧，奄有四方。

维此王季，帝度其心。貊^{mò}其德音，其德克明。克明克类，克长克君。王此大邦，

克顺克比。比于文王，其德靡悔。既受帝祉，施于孙子。

The Rise of Zhou

O God is great!
He saw our state,
Surveyed our land,
Saw how people did stand.
Dissatisfied
With Yin-Shang's side,
Then He would fain
Find out again.
Another state.
To rule its fate
His eyes turned west;
Our state was blessed.

Tai cut the head
Off the trunk dead
And hewed with blows
The bushy rows.
The rotten trees.
And mulberries
Were cleared away
Or put in array.
God made the road
For men's abode.
King Tai was made
Heaven's sure aide.

God visited Mount Qi
And thinned oak tree on tree.

Cypress and pines stood straight;
God founded the Zhou State.
He chose Tai as its head,
And Ji when Tai was dead.
Ji loved his brothers dear;
His heart was full of cheer.
When Ji was head of state,
He made its glory great.
The House of Zhou was blest
North to south, east to west.

God gave King Ji
The power to see
Clearly right from wrong
That he might rule for long.
With intelligence great
He could lead the whole state;
He ruled with wisdom high,
Thus obeyed far and nigh.
In his son King Wen's days
People still sang his praise.
For God's blessings would run
To his son and grandson.

To our King Wen God said,
"Don't let the foe invade
Your holy land with might;
First occupy the height."

The Mi tribe disobeyed,
On our land made a raid,
Attacked Yuan and Gong State;
King Wen's anger was great.
He sent his troops in rows
To stop invading foes
That the Zhou House might stand
And rule over the land.

The capital gave order
To attack from Yuan border
And occupy the height.
Let no foe come with might
Near our hill or our mountain
Nor to drink from our fountain
Nor our pools filled by rain.
King Wen surveyed the plain,
Settled and occupied
Hillside and riverside.
As great king he would stand
For people and the land.

To our King Wen God said,
"High virtue you've displayed.

You're ever lenient
To deal out punishment.
Making no effort on your part,
You follow me at heart. "
To our King Wen God said,
"Consult allied brigade,
Attack with brethren strong,
Use scaling ladders long
And engines of assault
To punish Chong tribe's fault. "

The engines of on-fall
Attacked the Chong State wall.
Many captives were ta'en
And left ears of the slain.
Sacrifice made afield,
We called the foe to yield.
The engines of on-fall
Destroyed the Chong State wall.
The foe filled with dismay,
Their forces swept away.
None dared insult Zhou State;
All obeyed our king great.

伟大的上天，威严地注视下方。

他观察四方，寻求百姓安定的主张。

他看见夏与商，不得民心就要亡。

上天环顾四方，思度谁能将这重任担当。

上天将择定一国，增加它的规模。

于是眷顾西土，此处适宜宅居。

拔除树木，清理枯木，修剪平整，灌木萌芽。

开辟道路，剪除柽木与椐木。

排除剔除，山桑黄桑。

上帝转向明德之君，犬戎部族落荒而逃。

上天选配合意之人，他受命于天江山稳固。

上帝省视岐山，柞树棫树皆除，唯有松柏耸立。

上帝建周国寻合宜之君，自太伯看到王季。

这位王季，对待朋友有真心，对待兄长似朋友。

他能让周邦有厚福，让老天赐他们无上荣光。

他们所受福禄永不消失，覆盖到四方。

这位王季，上帝度量他的心胸。

要将他的美德发扬光大，他的最显著的德行是明察是非。

他擅长分辨是非与善恶，能为长者与人君。

能够在这大邦做君王，人人和顺将他亲近。

他的权力传承到文王，德行高尚没有遗憾。

接受上帝的福祉，子孙受惠无穷止。

上帝对文王说，不要暴虐，不要将别人歆羡，要先上岸。

密人不肯恭顺，竟敢抗拒大国，从阮国侵犯到共国。

文王大怒，整顿军旅，阻击密人的进犯。

加固周之福祉，安定全天下。

依靠着镐京，撤出阮国边疆，登我之高岗。

不许陈兵我山陵，不管是大山还是小山。

不许饮我的泉水，那是我的泉水与池水。

重新规划山与原，决定定居岐山南，就在渭水旁。

我是万国榜样，是下民之王。

上帝告诉文王："我记着你的美德。对百姓不疾言厉色，不严刑峻法。让百姓感觉不到你的存在，这就顺应了帝王的准则。"

上帝还对文王说："多和友邦商量，联合兄弟之邦。用你攻城的钩援，与你的那些战车，去攻伐崇国的城墙。"

战车缓缓启动，崇国的城墙高耸。

抓来俘虏不断，割下耳朵让他们驯服。

出征和归来都要祭天，招降敌人安抚百姓，四方谁敢侮辱周邦。

战车轰隆，崇国城墙高耸。

征伐突袭，统统消灭。四方不敢再拂逆。

　　此诗是一首周部族的开国史诗，讲述了武王祖父王季和父亲文王的创业史。他们讨伐密人和崇国，一步步稳固地盘，收获人心，赢得天下。诗中依然一再强调这是上天的意思，让他们的行为天然地具有合理性。此诗包含对历史过程的叙述，对历史人物的塑造，对战争场面的描绘，可谓内容繁复，规模宏阔，笔力遒劲，具有较强的感染力和史诗性。

①耆：通"旨"，意旨，意图。②憎：通"增"。③安安：安顺，指驯服。

文王之什·灵台

经始灵台,经之营之。庶民攻之,不日成之。

经始勿亟,庶民子来。

王在灵囿,麀鹿攸伏。麀鹿濯濯,白鸟翯翯。

王在灵沼①,於牣鱼跃。

虞业维枞,贲鼓维镛。於论鼓钟,於乐辟廱。

於论鼓钟,於乐辟雍②。鼍鼓逢逢。蒙瞍奏公。

The Wondrous Park

When the tower began
To be built, every man
Took part as if up-heated,
The work was soon completed.
"No hurry," said the king,
But they worked as his offspring.

In Wondrous Park the king
Saw the deer in the ring
Lie at his left and right;
How sweet sang the birds white.
The king by Wondrous Pond

Saw fishes leap and bound.

In water-girded hall.
Beams were long and posts tall.
Drums would beat and bells ring
To amuse our great king.

Drums would beat and bells ring
To amuse our great king.
The lezard-skin drums beat;
Blind musicians sang sweet.

开始规划灵台，细细构思经营。
老百姓都来建造，没多久就已建成。
开始规划就不用着急，老百姓都会来帮忙。

君主在园林中，看到母鹿伏卧。
母鹿滋润肥硕，白鸟羽翼莹洁。
君主在那灵沼，啊，满池鱼欢喜跳跃。

架子已经搭好，悬挂着鼓与钟。
啊，钟鼓有序，啊，无限欢乐在离宫。

啊，钟鼓有序，啊，乐在离宫。
鳄鱼皮鼓砰砰有声，盲乐师演奏颂歌。

　　此诗是中国最早的表现园囿之美的诗歌。
周王的宫殿，犹如天堂，母鹿悠然自得，白
鸟羽翼如雪，连鱼儿都比别处欢快。钟鼓齐
奏，盲乐师献上颂歌，一切都是那么和谐。
特别是第三章后两句与第四章前两句的重复，
顶针修辞格的运用将游乐的热烈气氛渲染得
格外浓烈。

①於：叹词，啊。②辟廱：离宫。

文王之什·下武

下武维周，世有哲王。三后在天，王配于京。

王配于京，世德作求。永言配命，成王之孚。

成王之孚，下土之式。永言孝思，孝思维则。

媚兹一人，应侯顺德。永言孝思，昭哉嗣服。

昭兹来许，绳其祖武。於万斯年，受天之祜。

受天之祜，四方来贺。於万斯年，不遐有佐^①。

In Zhou successors rise;
All of them are kings wise.
To the three kings in heaven
King Wu in Hao is given.

King Wu in Hao is given
To the orders of Heaven.
He would seek virtue good
To attain true kinghood.

To attain true kinghood,
Be filial a man should.
He'd be pattern for all;
"Be filial" is his call.

All people love King Wu;
What they are told, they do.
Be filial a man should;
The bright successor's good.

All bright successor's good
Follow their fatherhood.
For long they will be given
The blessings of good Heaven.

The blessings of good Heaven
And good Earth will be given
For long yea's without end
To the people's great friend.

千秋万代唯有周朝，世代都有圣明之王。
三代君主像日月在天，同王受命在镐京。

周王受命在镐京，配得上祖德。
他的行为永远合乎天理，成就王者之信。

成就王者之信，是天下的榜样。
永记孝思这件事，孝思就是以先王为榜样。

多么美好这个新王，应当顺从祖宗之德。
永记孝思这件事，告诉后代要传承。

告诉所有的继承人，要延续祖宗的功绩。
啊，千秋万代，受老天之福。

受老天之福，四方来贺。
啊，千秋万代，谁会不来辅佐。

　　修身齐家治国平天下，以孝为根本，做到孝，余事也就一顺百顺了。这首诗是周康王继位时的颂歌，赞扬他的祖先，告诫他要对先王亦步亦趋，才能赢得四方辅佐。此诗结构严谨，层层递进，表现出流美谐婉的韵律。

①遐：通"何"。

文王之什·文王有声

文王有声，遹骏有声。遹求厥宁，遹观厥成。文王烝哉^①！

文王受命，有此武功。既伐于崇，作邑于丰。文王烝哉！

筑城伊淢，作丰伊匹。匪棘其欲，遹追来孝。王后烝哉！

王公伊濯，维丰之垣。四方攸同，王后维翰。王后烝哉！

丰水东注，维禹之绩。四方攸同^②，皇王维辟。皇王烝哉！

镐京辟雍，自西自东，自南自北，无思不服。皇王烝哉^③！

考卜维王，宅是镐京。维龟正之，武王成之。武王烝哉！

丰水有芑，武王岂不仕？诒厥孙谋，以燕翼子。武王烝哉！

Kings Wen and Wu

King Wen had a great fame
And famous he became.
He sought peace in the land
And saw it peaceful stand.
O King Wen was so grand!

King Wen whom gods did bless
Achieved martial success.
Having overthrown Chong,
He fixed his town at Feng.
O may King Wen live long!

King Wen built moat and wall
Around the capital
Not for his own desire.
But for those of his sire.
O our prince we admire!

King Wen at capital
Strong as the city wall,
The lords from state to state
Paid homage to prince great.
Our royal prince was great.

The River Feng east flowed;
Our thanks to Yu we owed.
The lords from land to land
Paid homage to king grand.
How great did King Wu stand!

He built water-girt hall
At Hao the capital.
North to south, east to west,
By people he was blest.
King Wu was at his crest.

The king divined the site;
The tortoise-shell foretold it right
To build the palace hall
At Hao the capital.
King Wu was admired by all.

By River Feng white millet grew.
How could talents not serve King Wu?
All that he'd planned and done
Was for the son and grandson.
King Wu was second to none.

四

鹤鸣九皋

文王有着好声誉，堪称宏大的好声誉。

他寻求天下安宁，终得见成功。美哉文王。

文王受天之命，所以有此武功。

他讨伐崇国，建造丰邑。美哉文王。

他修建护城河，作为丰京的守卫。

不济个人之欲，追念先祖的训导。美哉文王。

文王的功业恢弘，如高墙守护丰城。

四方都来归顺，文王是中流砥柱。美哉文王。

丰水东流，是禹的成绩。

四方归顺，周王是君主榜样，美哉武王。

镐京原是离宫，自西自东，自南自北，没有谁不服从。美哉武王。

我王占卜，定居镐京。

神龟确定，武王成之。美哉武王。

丰水洋洋水草，武王在此难道无事可做？

他不过是要为子孙谋，庇护后代安定。美哉武王。

　　文王"作邑于丰"，武王"宅是镐京"：两代父子接力，终于有了赫赫周朝。然而，也不过是为子孙谋，成就他们自家的事业。此诗依照时间顺序谋篇布局，叙事与抒情结合，巧妙运用比兴手法，用韵富于变化，具有较高的艺术成就。

①烝：美。②王后：指文王。③皇王：指武王。

酌之用匏。食之饮之，君之宗之。

笃公刘，既溥既长。既景乃冈，相其阴阳，观其流泉。其军三单，度其隰原。

彻田为粮，度其夕阳。豳居允荒。

笃公刘，于豳斯馆。涉渭为乱②，取厉取锻，止基乃理。爰众爰有，夹其皇涧。

溯其过涧。止旅乃密，芮鞫之即。

生民之什·公刘

①笃公刘，匪居匪康。乃埸乃疆，乃积乃仓；乃裹餱粮，于橐于囊。思辑用光，

弓矢斯张；干戈戚扬，爰方启行。

笃公刘，于胥斯原。既庶既繁，既顺乃宣，而无永叹。陟则在巘，复降在原。

何以舟之？维玉及瑶，鞞琫容刀。

笃公刘，逝彼百泉。瞻彼溥原，乃陟南冈。乃觏于京，京师之野。于时处处，

于时庐旅，于时言言，于时语语。

笃公刘，于京斯依。跄跄济济，俾筵俾几。既登乃依，乃造其曹。执豕于牢，

Duke Liu

Duke Liu was blessed;
He took nor ease nor rest.
He divided the fields
And stored in barns the yields.
In bags and sacks he tied
Up grain and meat when dried.
He led people in rows,
With arrows and drawn bows.
With axes, shields and spears,
They marched on new frontiers.

Duke Liu would fain
Survey a fertile plain
For his people to stay.
On that victorious day
No one would sigh nor rest.
He came up mountain-crest
And descended again.
We saw his girdle then
Adorned with gems and jade,
His precious sword displayed.

Duke Liu crossed the mountains
And saw a hundred fountains.
He surveyed the plain wide
By the southern hillside.
He found a new capital
Wide for his people all.
Some thought it good for the throng;
Others would not dwell there for long.

There was discussion free;
They talked in high glee.

Duke Liu was blessed;
At capital he took rest,
Put stools on mats he spread
For officers he led.
They leant on stools and sat
On the ornamented mat.
A penned pig was killed;
Their gourds with wine were filled.
They were well drunk and fed;
All hailed him as state head.

Duke Liu would fain
Measure the hill and plain
Broad and long; he surveyed
Streams and springs, light and shade;
His three armies were placed
By the hillside terraced;
He measured plains anew
And fixed the revenue.
Fields were tilled in the west;
The land of Bin was blessed.

Duke Liu who wore the crown
At Bin had settled down.
He crossed the River Wei
To gather stones by day.
All boundaries defined,

People worked with one mind
On the Huang Riverside
Towards Guo River wide.
The people dense would stay
On the shore of the Ney.

坚定的公刘，不肯安居。

给农田划分疆界，将粮食收进谷仓。

他裹了干粮，放进大的小的袋中。

团结大众显国荣光，将弓箭开张。

拿起干戈斧钺，开始踏上征程。

坚定的公刘，审视这片平原。

百姓人心所向，齐齐跟从，而无喟叹。

登上小山坡，再下到平原。

随身携带什么？无非美玉和宝石，还有饰物上面的佩刀。

坚定的公刘，去看那泉水。

遥望平原，又登南冈。

望向那京师，以及京师之郊野。

于是安居，于是羁旅，于是谈天，于是笑语。

坚定的公刘，定居在京师。

群臣众多而有礼，按照秩序入席。

大家登席凭几，然后告祭猪神。

猪圈里逮猪下酒，喝酒就用那大瓢。

有吃有喝心欢喜，共推公刘为宗主。

坚定的公刘，疆土既广又长。

在山岗上测量日影，观察那阴阳，观察泉的流向。

让手下的兵士三班轮换，将低湿的原野测量。

开垦荒地种粮，看着那夕阳，豳的土地广袤。

坚定的公刘，在豳原建造馆舍。

他横渡渭水采石料，有磨石也有锤石。

他定下基地，治理田地。

人口增加，物产丰富，沿着皇涧，面向过涧，皆是人群。

定居的人们，住满河岸。

公刘姓姬名刘，"公"为尊称。传说他是后稷之后，是周部落的先祖。他原本可以在邰城安居，却"匪居匪康"，开疆拓土，建邦立国，不屈不挠地达成理想抱负，所以用一个"笃"——一心一意——来形容他再合适不过了。此诗既赞扬了公刘作为领导者所拥有的深谋远虑与开拓进取的精神，又颂扬了公刘与民众齐心协力与患难与共的光辉形象。

①笃：忠诚。引申为一心一意。②乱：横渡。

生民之什·洞酌

洞酌彼行潦，挹彼注兹，可以饎。岂弟君子，
民之父母。

洞酌彼行潦，挹彼注兹，可以濯罍。岂弟君子，
民之攸归。

洞酌彼行潦，挹彼注兹，可以濯溉。岂弟君子，
民之攸塈。

Take Water from Far Away

Take water from pools far away,
Pour it in vessels that it may
Be used to steam millet and rice.
A prince should give fraternal advice
Like parent to his people nice.

Take water from pools far away,
Pour it in vessels that it may
Be used to wash the spirit-vase.

A prince should give fraternal praise
To his people for better days.

Take water from pools far away,
Pour it in vessels that it may
Be used to cleanse everything.
To our fraternal prince or king
Like water his people will cling.

　　　　远远地走到小溪旁，舀起溪水入水缸，可以蒸
煮出好滋味。
　　　　温和的君子，是百姓之父母。

　　　　远远地走到小溪旁，舀起溪水入水缸，可以洗
涤酒坛。
　　　　温和的君子，让人民有所归依。

　　　　远远地走到小溪旁，舀起溪水入水缸，可以洗
涤酒器。
　　　　温和的君子，让人民安心归附。

　　这时一首歌颂领导者能得民心的诗。老
子说，上善若水，水利万物而不争。君主手中
握有生杀予夺之权，若是能够温和如水，让人
民有实在的好处，才能得到百姓的真心拥戴。

凤凰于飞，翙翙其羽，亦傅于天。蔼蔼王多吉人，维君子命，媚于庶人。

凤凰鸣矣，于彼高冈。梧桐生矣，于彼朝阳。菶菶萋萋，雍雍喈喈。

君子之车，既庶且多。君子之马，既闲且驰。④矢诗不多，维以⑤遂歌。

生民之什·卷阿

有卷者阿，飘风自南。岂弟君子，来游来歌，以矢其音。

伴奂尔游矣，优游尔休矣。岂弟君子，俾尔弥尔性①②，似先公酋矣。

尔土宇昄章，亦孔之厚矣。岂弟君子，俾尔弥尔性，百神尔主矣。

尔受命长矣，茀禄尔康矣。岂弟君子，俾尔弥尔性，纯嘏尔常矣。

有冯有翼，有孝有德，以引以翼。岂弟君子，四方为则。③

颙颙卬卬，如圭如璋，令闻令望。岂弟君子，四方为纲。

凤凰于飞，翙翙其羽，亦集爰止。蔼蔼王多吉士，维君子使，媚于天子。

King Cheng's Progress

The mountain undulates;
The southern breeze vibrates.
Here our fraternal king
Comes crooning and wandering;
In praise of him I sing.

You're wandering with pleasure
Or taking rest at leisure.
O fraternal king, hear!
May you pursue the career
Of your ancestors dear!

Your territory's great
And secure is your state.
O fraternal king, hear!
May you pursue your career
As host of gods whom you revere!

For long you're Heaven-blessed;
You enjoy peace and rest.
O fraternal king, hear!
May you pursue your career
And be blessed far and near!

You've supporters and aides
Virtuous of all grades
To lead or act as wing.
O our fraternal king,
Of your pattern all sing,

Majestic you appear,
Like jade-mace without peer;

You're praised from side to side.
O fraternal king, hear!
Of the state you're the guide.

Phoenixes fly
With rustling wings
And settle high.
Officers of the king's
Employed each one
To please the Heaven's Son.

Phoenixes fly
With rustling wings
To azure sky.
Officers of the king's
At your command
Please people of the land.

Phoenixes sing
On lofty height;
Planes grow in spring
On morning bright.
Lush are plane-trees;
Phoenixes sing at ease.

O many are
Your cars and steed;
Your steed and car
Run at high speed.
I sing but to prolong
Your holy song.

诗三百·思无邪

鹤鸣九皋

山陵起起伏伏，旋风从南而来。

温和儒雅的君子，到此游览作歌，大家都向君子献歌。

闲暇悠游，以悠游为休息。

温和儒雅的君子，终生劳作何所求，继承祖业千秋。

你的封疆版图，辽阔无垠。

温和儒雅的君子，终生劳作有作为，是天地山川鬼神之主。

你受天命长久矣，福禄安康归你有。

温和儒雅的君子，终生劳作百岁寿，福禄常拥有。

可以依靠可以辅佐，有孝心又有美德，有人在前引导，有人左右庇护。

温和儒雅的君子，四方以你为楷模。

庄重又纯洁，如圭如璋，是你的美誉与威仪。

温和儒雅的君子，是天下人的榜样。

凤凰高飞，扇动它的翅膀，所当止时，停在树上。

王你身边贤士云集，供你驱遣，爱戴你这天子。

凤凰高飞，扇动它的翅膀，直上天际。

王你身边贤士云集，听从你的指令，爱护四方百姓。

凤凰长鸣，于彼高冈。

梧桐生矣，于彼朝阳。

梧桐茂密莘莘萋萋，凤凰鸣叫雍雍喈喈。

君子的车，华美且多。

君子的马，娴熟地奔驰。

我们献上这么多诗篇，为了答谢而歌。

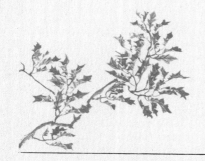

此诗借游宴对周王歌颂功德,《大雅》
里歌颂君主有不同的角度,这篇突出"凯弟"
也就是诗中的"岂弟"二字,即温和。君主
温和儒雅,能听得进人言,所以贤德之人真
心爱戴他,各方面给予辅佐,让他能够车马
悠游,整首诗洋溢着雍容祥和的盛世之象。
此诗结构完整,意象谐和,语言精练,赋笔
之外,兼用比兴,其艺术手法的运用对后世
产生了广泛的影响。

①弥:终。②性:命。③冯:可依者。④矢诗不多:矢,献;不,助词,无意义。诗
歌很多。⑤遂:答。

无俾正败。戎虽小子，而式弘大。

民亦劳止，汔可小安。惠此中国，国无有残。无纵诡随，以谨缱绻。式遏寇虐，无俾正反。王欲玉女，是用大谏。

生民之什·民劳

民亦劳止，汔可小康。惠此中国，以绥四方。无纵诡随，以谨无良。式遏寇虐，憯不畏明。柔远能迩，以定我王。

民亦劳止，汔可小休。惠此中国，以为民逑。无纵诡随，以谨惽恢。式遏寇虐，无俾民忧。无弃尔劳，以为王休。

民亦劳止，汔可小息。惠此京师，以绥四国。无纵诡随，以谨罔极。式遏寇虐，无俾作慝。敬慎威仪，以近有德。

民亦劳止，汔可小愒。惠此中国，俾民忧泄。无纵诡随，以谨丑厉。式遏寇虐，

The People Are Hard Pressed

The people are hard pressed;
They need a little rest.
Do the Central Plain good,
You'll reign o'er neighborhood.
Of the wily beware;
Against the vice take care!
Put the oppressors down
Lest they fear not the crown.
Show kindness far and near;
Consolidate your sphere.

The people are hard pressed;
They need repose and rest.
Do the Central Plain good,
People will come from neighborhood.
Of the wily beware;
Against bad men take care!
Repress those who oppress;
Relive those in distress.
Through loyal service done
The royal quiet is won.

The people are hard pressed;
They need relief and rest.
Do good in the capital,
You'll please your people all.
Of the wily beware;

Against wicked men take care!
Repress those who oppress
Lest they go to excess.
In manner dignified
You'll have good men at your side.

The people are hard pressed;
They need some ease and rest.
Do good in Central Plain
To relieve people's pain.
Of the wily beware;
Against evil take care!
Put the oppressors down
Lest your rule be o'erthrown.
Though still young in the State,
What you can do is great.

The people are hard pressed;
They need quiet and rest.
Do good in Central Plain
Lest people suffer pain.
Of the wily beware;
Of flattery take care!
Put the oppressors down
Lest the state be o'erthrown.
O king, as jade you're nice.
Please take my frank frank advice!

鹤鸣九皋

百姓真是太辛苦，请让他们稍稍休息。

让京师受益，可使四方安宁。

不要放纵奸诈的歹人，提防无良之辈。

要遏制压榨残害百姓的人，不怕坏人手段强。

要能温和地对待远近之人，才能安定我王的功业。

百姓真是太辛苦，请让他们稍稍休息。

让京师受益，可使百姓安居。

不要放纵奸诈的歹人，提防作乱之辈。

要遏制压榨残害百姓的人，不要让百姓忧虑。

不要放弃从前的功劳，让我王可以休息。

百姓真是太辛苦，请让他们稍稍休息。

让京师受益，可使四方安宁。

不要放纵奸诈的歹人，提防行为不端之辈。

要遏制压榨残害百姓的人，不要作恶。

端庄而又讲礼仪，才能接近于贤德。

百姓真是太辛苦，请让他们稍稍休息。

让京师受益，可使百姓无忧。

不要放纵奸诈的歹人，要提防丑恶之辈。

要遏制压榨残害百姓的人，不要让政事败坏。

你虽然是个年轻人，但是可担大任。

百姓真是太辛苦，请让他们稍稍休息。

让京师受益，国内没有隐患。

不要放纵奸诈的歹人，提防他们结党营私。

要遏制压榨残害百姓的人，不要让政局翻覆。

我王，想要成就你，才使劲劝谏你。

　　此诗是一首具有古风意味的文人作品。《诗序》说《民劳》是召穆公刺厉王之作。周厉王暴虐，致使百姓生活极度困苦。召穆公屡屡劝谏他，要体恤民力，改弦更张。这首诗更是提出具体方案，与民休息，维护京师，不亲近奸诈之人。

天之方懠。无为夸毗。威仪卒迷，善人载尸。民之方殿屎，则莫我敢葵？丧乱蔑资，曾莫惠我师？

天之牖民，如埙如篪，如璋如圭，如取如携。携无曰益③，牖民孔易。民之多辟④，无自立辟。

价人维藩，大师维垣，大邦维屏，大宗维翰，怀德维宁，宗子维城。无俾城坏，无独斯畏。

敬天之怒，无敢戏豫。敬天之渝，无敢驰驱。昊天曰明，及尔出王。昊天曰旦，及尔游衍。

生民之什·板

上帝板板，下民卒瘅。出话不然，为犹不远。靡圣管管，不实于亶。犹之未远，是用大谏。

天之方难，无然宪宪①。天之方蹶，无然泄泄②。辞之辑矣，民之洽矣。辞之怿矣，民之莫矣。

我虽异事，及尔同僚。我即尔谋，听我嚣嚣。我言维服，勿以为笑。先民有言，询于刍荛。

天之方虐，无然谑谑。老夫灌灌，小子蹻蹻ｊｉǎｏ。匪我言耄，尔用忧谑。多将熇熇，不可救药。

Censure

God won't our kingdom bless;
People are in distress.
Your words incorrect are,
Your plans cannot reach far.
You care not what sages do;
What you say is not true.
Your plans are far from nice;
So I give you advice.

Heaven sends troubles down.
O how can you not frown?
It makes turmoil prevail;
You talk to no avail.
If what you say is right,
'Twill be heard with delight.
If what you say is not,
It will soon be forgot.

Our duties different,
We serve the government.
I give you advice good;
Your attitude is rude.
My advice is sought after;
It's no matter for laughter.
Ancient saying is good:
"Consult cutters of wood! "

Heaven is doing wrong.
How can you get along?
I'm an old lord sincere.
How can you proud appear?

I'm not proud of my age.
How can you tease a sage?
Trouble will grow like fire,
Beyond remedy when higher.

Heaven's anger displayed,
Don't cajole nor upbraid!
The good and dignified
Are mute as men who died.
The people groan and sigh,
But none dare to ask why.
Wild disorder renewed,
Who'd help our multitude?

Heaven helps people mute
By whistle as by flute,
As two maces form one,
As something brought when done.
Bring anything you please,
You'll help people with ease.
They've troubles to deplore.
Don't give them any more!

Good men a fence install;
The people form a wall.
Screens are formed by each state
And each family great.
Virtue secures repose,
Walled up by kinsmen close.
Do not destroy the wall;
Be not lonely after all!

*

Revere great Heaven's ire
And do not play with fire!
Revere great Heaven gay
And don't drive your own way.
There's nought but Heaven knows;
It's with you where you go,
Great Heaven sees all clear;
It's with you where you appear.

上天反常，下民遭殃。

你说出话来不算数，做的谋划不长远。

背弃圣人不靠谱，诚信两字丢一边。

做的谋划不长远，是以此诗来劝谏。

老天正非难人世，别再喜气洋洋。

老天正酝酿动乱，别再漫不经心。

政令若是温和，百姓自然融洽；

政令若是败坏，民间就像生了大病。

我们虽职务不同，毕竟在做同一件事。

我跟你商量国事，你充耳不闻自说自话；

我跟你讨论事实，你不要再当成玩笑。

先人曾说过："有事可以请教割草打柴之人。"

老天正要虐这人间，你不要再开玩笑。

老夫何其忠诚，小子没有正形。

不是我说话老糊涂，你到这会儿还嬉皮笑脸。

你要是再这么火上浇油，接下来就会不可救药。

老天正在发怒，不要继续谄媚。

礼仪乱七八糟，好人如同行尸走肉。

老百姓正在呻吟，我不敢乱猜想。

丧乱导致没钱，没有办法安抚百姓。

老天开启民智，就像吹埙吹篪之和洽，就像璋和圭之和谐，就像取和携之统一。

提携起来全无关隘，开启民智多么容易。

民间已经有那么多麻烦事，不要再给自己找麻烦。

好人就像藩篱，百姓就像围墙。

大国就像屏障，大族就像柱梁。

怀有美德就能安宁，宗子就像围城。

不要让这城墙坏，不要孤立无援只能白白害怕。

敬畏老天的怒气，不要再笑嘻嘻。

敬畏老天的色变，不要再放纵自己。

老天眼明心亮，就像和你共同出入。

老天心知肚明，就像和你一起游荡。

这首诗的主旨据说是召伯刺周厉王，诗中确实有老臣的苦心和无能为力，堪比《出师表》。其实，看具体文辞，更加疾言厉色，更像是苦心孤诣的老臣面对那恃宠而骄的天子新宠，虽有一腔怒火但是又无能为力，只有借老天的名义威慑之。此诗劝说和警告并用兼施，使言事说理更为透彻，流露出作者忧国忧民的一片拳拳之心。

①宪宪：欣欣。②泄泄：多言多语。③益：通"隘"，阻碍。④辟：邪僻。

以事一人。

人亦有言，柔则茹之，刚则吐之。维仲山甫，柔亦不茹，刚亦不吐。不侮矜寡，不畏强御。

人亦有言，德輶如毛，民鲜克举之。我仪图之，维仲山甫举之。爱莫助之。

衮职有阙，维仲山甫补之。

仲山甫出祖，四牡业业。征夫捷捷，每怀靡及。四牡彭彭，八鸾锵锵。王命仲山甫，城彼东方。

四牡骙骙，八鸾喈喈。仲山甫徂齐，式遄其归。吉甫作诵，穆如清风。仲山甫永怀，以慰其心。

荡之什·烝民

天生烝民，有物有则。民之秉彝①，好是懿德。天监有周，昭假于下。保兹天子，生仲山甫。

仲山甫之德，柔嘉维则。令仪令色，小心翼翼。古训是式，威仪是力。天子是若，明命使赋。

王命仲山甫，式是百辟，缵戎祖考，王躬是保。出纳王命，王之喉舌。赋政于外，四方爰发。

肃肃王命，仲山甫将之。邦国若否，仲山甫明之。既明且哲，以保其身。夙夜匪解，

Premier Shan Fu

Heaven who made mankind
Endowed him with body and mind.
The people loved manhood.
Could they not love the good?
Heaven beheld our crown
And shed light up and down.
To help His son on earth,
To Shan Fu he gave birth.

Cadet Shan Fu is good,
Endowed with mild manhood.
Dignified is his air;
He behaves with great care,
He follows lessons old;
He is as strong as bold.
He follows Heaven's Son
That his orders may be done.

The king orders him to appear.
As pattern to each peer;
To serve as his ancestors dear
And protect the king here;
To give orders to old and young
And be the king's throat and tongue;
To spread decrees and orders
That they be obeyed on four borders.

The orders dignified
Are spread out far and wide.
Premier Shan Fu does know

The kingdom's weal and woe.
He's wise and free from blame,
To guard his life and fame.
He's busy night and day
To serve the king for aye.

As people have said oft,
"We choose to eat the soft.
The hard will be cast out. "
On this Shan Fu cast doubt.
He won't devour the soft;
Nor is the hard cast oft.
He'll do the weak no wrong,
Nor will he fear the strong.

People say everywhere,
"Virtue is light as air;
But few can hold it high. "
I ponder with a sigh:
Only Shan Fu can hold it high
And needs no help from the sky.
When the king has defect,
Shan Fu helps him correct.

Where Shan Fu goes along,
Run his four horses strong.
His men alert would find
They often lag behind.
His four steeds run east-bound
To eight bells' tinkling sound.

四 鹤鸣九皋

*

The king orders him to go down
To fortify the eastern town.

His four steeds galloping,
His eight bells gaily ring.
Shan Fu goes to Qi state;
His return won't be late.
I, Ji Fu, make this song
To blow like breeze for long.
O Shan Fu, though we part,
My song will soothe your heart.

天生万民，每样事物都有准则。

百姓遵守的常理，是爱好美德。

老天看顾周朝，将昭明之德置于下方。

为了保佑这天子，生出仲山甫来。

仲山甫之德，以柔嘉为准则。

好仪态与好脸色，看上去小心翼翼。

以古训为范式，勉力遵从法度。

天子选择了他，明命他颁布政令。

天子命令仲山甫，给百官做榜样。

继承你祖宗功业，辅佐天子终生。

出入承布王命，是为王之喉舌。

对外颁布王政，四方诸侯呼应。

王命何其庄严，仲山甫来奉行。

国事是否顺利，仲山甫心知肚明。

他坦荡又智慧，足以保其身。

白天黑夜不懈，皆为天子一人。

人家经常这么说：柔弱就有人欺负，刚硬就有人避让。

只有仲山甫，他不欺弱者，也不避让强者。

不欺负鳏寡，也不害怕强敌。

人家经常这么说：美德轻如鸿毛，但很少有人能举起它。

我细细思度这句话，只有仲山甫能举起它。

爱莫助之。

天子礼服破败，仲山甫补之。

仲山甫出门行祭，四匹马健壮。

征夫脚步轻捷，总忧事儿不能完成。

四匹马疾行，八卦鸾铃响锵锵。

王命仲山甫，筑城于东方。

四匹马飞奔，八个鸾铃响嚌嚌。

仲山甫前往齐地，车子拉着他速速归。

吉甫作歌吟诵，深长如清风。

仲山甫多记挂，让我这首诗来安慰你的心。

　　周宣王派重臣仲山甫去齐地筑城，此诗为临行时尹吉甫所作。全诗章法整饬，表达灵活，是后世送别诗之祖。仲山甫为人柔嘉，不欺软怕硬。诗中金句是："德辅如毛，民鲜克举之。"美德虽然轻如鸿毛，但人被自身欲望左右，无法做到，只有这位仲山甫，总是保持着了不起的平衡。所以他一旦出游，大家都会深为记挂，此诗赞扬仲山甫的美德与辅佐宣王的政绩，流露出仲山甫深受周人的爱戴和尊崇。

①秉彝：秉，执守。彝，常理。

鹤鸣九皋

不显其光。诸娣从之，祁祁如云。韩侯顾之，烂其盈门。

蹶父孔武，靡国不到。为韩姞相攸，莫如韩乐。孔乐韩土，川泽訏訏，鲂鱮甫甫，

麀鹿噳噳，有熊有罴，有猫有虎。庆既令居，韩姞燕誉。

溥彼韩城，燕师所完。以先祖受命，因时百蛮。王锡韩侯，其追其貊。奄受北国，

因以其伯。实墉实壑，实亩实藉。献其貔皮，赤豹黄罴。

荡之什·韩奕

奕奕梁山，维禹甸之，有倬其道。韩侯受命，王亲命之：缵戎祖考，无废朕命。

夙夜匪解，虔共尔位，朕命不易。①干不庭方，以佐戎辟。

四牡奕奕，孔脩且张。韩侯入觐，以其介圭，入觐于王。王锡韩侯，淑旂绥章，

簟茀错衡，玄衮赤舄，钩膺镂锡，鞹鞃浅幭miè，鞗革金厄。

韩侯出祖，出宿于屠。显父饯之，清酒百壶。其肴维何？炰鳖鲜鱼。其蔌维何？

维笋及蒲。其赠维何？乘马路车。笾豆有且，侯氏燕胥。

韩侯取妻，②汾王之甥，③蹶父之子。韩侯迎止，于蹶之里。百两彭彭，八鸾锵锵，

The Marquis of Han

The Liang Mountains are grand;
Yu of Xia cultivated the land.
The Marquis of Han came his way
To be invested in array.
"Serve as your fathers had done, "
In person said the Heaven's Son,
"Do not belie our trust;
Show active zeal you must.
Let things be well arranged;
Let no order be changed.
Assist us to extort.
Lords who won't come to court. "

His cab was drawn by four steeds
Long and large, running high speeds.
The marquis at court did stand,
His mace of rank in hand.
He bowed to Heaven's Son,
Who showed him his gifts one by one.
The dragon flags all new
And screens made of bamboo,
Black robes and slippers red,
Carved hooks for horse's head,
A tiger's skin aboard
And golden rings for the lord.

The marquis went on homeward way
At Tu for the night he did stay.
Xian Fu invited him to dine,
Drinking a hundred vases of wine.
What were the viands in the dishes?
Roast turtles and fresh fishes.
And what was the ragout?
Tender shoots of bamboo.
What were the gifts furthermore?
A cab of state and horses four.
So many were the dishes fine,
The marquis with delight did dine.

The marquis was to wed
The king's niece in nuptial bed.
It was the daughter of Gui Fu
The marquis came to woo.
A hundred cabs came on the way
To Gui's house in array.
Eight bells made tinkling sound,
Shedding glory around.
Virgins followed the bride in crowd
As beautiful as cloud.
The marquis looked round
The house in splendor drowned.

Gui Fu in war had fame.
Among the states whence he came,
He liked Han by the water,
Where he married his daughter.
In Han there are large streams
Full of tenches and breams;
The deer and doe are mild
And tigers and cats wild;
The bears or black or brown
Roam the land up and down.
His daughter Ji lived there;
She found no state more fair.

鹤鸣九皋

The city wall of Han
Was built by people of Yan.
han ancestors got orders
To rule o'er tribes on borders.
The marquis has below.
Him tribes of Zhai and Mo.
He should preside as chief
Of northern states and fief;
Lay out fields, make walls strong
And dig deep moats along;
Present skins of bears brown
And fox white to the crown.

梁山巍峨，大禹治之，它有大道光明。

韩侯入京受命，周王命之：继承你祖先的事业，勿忘我的命令。

白天黑夜不松懈，忠诚于你的职位。

我的任命不会改变。去讨伐不朝见我的诸侯，以此辅佐你的君主。

四匹高头大马，身材何其修长。

韩侯入京朝见，捧着他的封圭，去拜见那周王。

周王赐予韩侯：

龙旗杆头挑羽毛，竹帘车子金横木，黑色礼服赤色靴，饰物华丽绕马身，浅色虎皮覆车轼，皮绳金环绕辔头。

韩侯出祭路神，途中宿于屠地。

显父为他饯行，端上清酒百壶。

荤菜是啥，烹煮鳖鱼。

蔬菜是啥，有笋有蒲。

送了他啥？驷马高车。

食器堆叠，韩侯安乐。

韩侯娶妻，厉王的外甥女，蹶父的女儿。

韩侯迎娶，来到蹶邑。

百辆大车排长队，八个鸾铃响锵锵，多么排场风光。

陪嫁姑娘随其后，翩翩多如云锦。

韩侯回首望之，灿烂光辉盈门。

蹶父孔武有力，没有国家不曾去。

他为韩姞寻归宿，韩国堪称乐土。

多么快乐的韩土，川泽浩瀚，鲂鱮肥美，公鹿母鹿鸣嗷嗷，有熊有罴，有猫有虎。

庆祝得到好居处，韩姞安乐又欢喜。

韩城广大，燕族筑成。

因为先祖受命，统治蛮族。

天子赐韩侯继承祖业，追族与貊族都在你手中。

全面节制整个北国，作为诸族的首领。

去筑城，去挖沟，去耕田，去收税。

他们贡献白狐皮，还有赤豹与黄熊。

　　君主想守护好江山，很重要的一点就是安顿好诸侯，恩威并施，既不能宽纵，也不能严苛。这首诗描述的是周宣王驾驭韩侯，给他很多赏赐，还把外甥女嫁给他，但也要求他忠于职守，兢兢业业镇守，能够成为北方的屏障，可谓用心良苦。此诗脉络连贯，层次清晰，语言风格变化多姿。

①干不庭方：干：讨伐。不庭方：不朝拜之国。②汾王：固厉王。③蹶父：周宣王的卿士。

鳌尔圭瓒，秬鬯一卣。告于文人，锡山土田。于周受命，自召祖命，虎拜稽首：

天子万年！

虎拜稽首，对扬王休。作召公考：天子万寿！明明天子，令闻不已。矢其文德，

洽此四国。

荡之什·汉江

江汉浮浮，武夫滔滔。匪安匪游，淮夷来求。既出我车，既设我旟。匪安匪舒，

淮夷来铺。

江汉汤汤，武夫洸洸。经营四方，告成于王。四方既平，王国庶定。时靡有争，

王心载宁。

江汉之浒，王命召虎：式辟四方，彻我疆土。匪疚匪棘，王国来极。于疆于理，

至于南海。

江汉之浒，王命召虎：来旬来宣。文武受命，召公维翰。无曰予小子，召公是似。肇敏戎公，

王命召虎：来旬来宣。文武受命，召公维翰。无曰予小子，召公是似。肇敏戎公，

用锡尔祉。

Duke Mu of Shao

Onward the rivers roared;
Forward our warriors poured.
There was no rest far and nigh.
We marched on River Huai.
Our cars drove on the way
Our flags flew on display.
There was no peace far and nigh;
We marched on tribes of Huai.

Onward the rivers flow;
Backward our warriors go.
The State reduced to order,
We come back from the border.
There is peace east and west;
North and south there is rest.
An end is put to the strife;
The king may live a peaceful life.

On the two rivers' borders
The king gives Shao Hu orders:
"Open up countryside
And land and fields divide.
Let people rule their fate
And conform to our State.
Define lands by decree
As far as southern sea. "

The king gives Shao Hu orders
To inspect southern borders;
"When Wen and Wu were kings,
Your ancestors were their wings.
Say not young you appear;
Do as your fathers dear.
You have well served the state;
I'll give you favor great. "

"Here is a cup of jade
And wine of millet made
Tell your ancestors grand
I'll confer on you more land.
I'll gratify your desires
As my sire did your sire's. "
Hu bows aground to say:
"May Heaven's Son live for aye! "

Hu bows aground again
In praise of royal reign.
He engraves Duke Shao's song,
Wishing the king live long.
The Heaven's Son is wise;
His endless fame will rise.
His virtue is so great
That he'll rule o'er every state.

江汉浮浮，将士如江水滔滔。

不偷安也不游荡，去将淮夷征讨。

出动我的战车，张开我的旗帜。

不偷安也不迟疑，陈师那淮夷。

江汉汤汤，将士像水波动荡。

经营四方，告成于周王。

四方既平，国家安定。

没有战争，王心安宁。

在江汉水边，周王命令召虎。

开辟四方，开发我疆土。

不要伤害他们，也不要逼迫他们，按照国家的准则来。

划出疆域，整理田畦，直到南海。

周王命令召虎：去巡查去宣布。

想当年文王武王皆受天命，召公是那栋梁。

你别说"我是小子"，召公的事业你要继承。

快谋划你的功绩，我会将福禄赐你。

赐你玉柄酒勺，赐你黑黍酿成的酒。

告诉拟公文的人，赐你山地和田亩。

到岐周受命，用你祖先那样的封典。

召虎下拜叩首，祈祝天子万年。

召虎下拜叩首，颂扬王之美。

写下一篇召公考，祝福天子万寿。

清明的天子，美誉无休止，布施他的美德，让四方融洽。

召虎听令率兵，开辟疆土，平定淮夷之乱，周宣王予以嘉奖和赏赐。虽然仍然以颂扬为主旨，但这首诗写得很有场景感。"江汉浮浮，武夫滔滔"，一看就是得胜之师的气象。周宣王用召虎祖上的功业鼓励他，并且赐予他美酒土地，让召虎获得精神与物质上的双重满足。同时，召虎又制作铜簋，告其先祖，颂扬天子，宣扬文德。此诗表现出君臣共求中兴的美好愿望。

王旅啴啴，如飞如翰。如江如汉，如山之苞。如川之流，绵绵翼翼。不测不克，

濯征徐国。

王犹允塞，徐方既来。徐方既同，天子之功。四方既平，徐方来庭。徐方不回，

王曰还归。

荡之什·常武

赫赫明明。王命卿士，南仲大祖，大师皇父。整我六师，以脩我戎。既敬既戒，

惠此南国。

三事就绪。

王谓尹氏，命程伯休父，左右陈行，戒我师旅。率彼淮浦，省此徐土。不留不处，

赫赫业业，有严天子。王舒保作，匪绍匪游。徐方绎骚，震惊徐方。如雷如霆，

徐方震惊。

王奋厥武，如震如怒。进厥虎臣，阚如虓虎。铺敦淮濆，仍执丑虏。截彼淮浦，

王师之所。

Expedition against Xu

Grand and wise is the sovereign who
Gave charge to Minister
And Grand-master Huang Fu,
Of whom Nan Zhong was ancestor.
"Put my six armies in order
And ready for warfare.
Set out for southern border.
With vigilance and care!"

The king told Yin to assign
The task to Count Xiu Fu
To march his troops in line
And in vigilance too;
To go along the river shore
Until they reach the land of Xu;
And not to stay there any more
When the three tasks get through.

How dignified and grand
Did the Son of Heaven show!
He advanced on the land
Nor too fast nor too slow.
The land of Xu was stirred
And greatly terrified
As if a thunder heard
Shook the land far and wide.

The king in brave array
Struck the foe with dismay.
His chariots went before
Like tigers did men roar.
Along the riverside
They captured the foes terrified.
They advanced to the rear
And occupied their sphere.

The legions of the king's
Are swift as birds on wings.
Like rivers they are long;
Like mountains they are strong.
They roll on like the stream;
Boundless and endless they seem.
Invincible, unfathomable, great,
They've conquered the Xu State.

The king has wisely planned
How to conquer Xu's land.
Xu's chiefs come to submit
All through the king's merit.
The country pacified,
Xu's chiefs come to the king's side,
They won't again rebel;
The king says, "All is well."

*

我王威武又英明。

我王任命卿士，在太祖庙里封南仲，太师皇父同听命。

整顿我六师，修理我兵器。警戒我兵士，让南国安宁。

王对尹氏说，命令程伯大司马，士卒左右列好队。

警戒我之军旅，率领他们赴淮浦，省视徐土。不要停留此处，任命完三卿就回转。

威仪赫赫向前，天子多么威严。

王师安缓慢慢行，徐国已起大骚动。

震惊徐国，像是听到雷霆，徐国震惊。

我王奋发展示其威武，如震如怒。

进军如猛虎，就像猛虎嘶吼。

军队陈列河堤上，抓获敌方俘虏。

切断敌军在淮浦，王师驻扎此处。

王师气势恢宏，像鸟群疾飞于天。

像江汉浩瀚无边，像大山不可动摇，像奔流直下之川。

连绵不绝，难以预测难战胜，征伐徐国。

王的谋划切合实际，徐国已经顺服。

徐国已经认同，这是天子之功。

四方既然平定，徐国前来朝见。

徐国不敢再违王命，周王说我们可以回朝。

周王御驾亲征，去讨伐徐国，平定叛乱。他选好统帅，训练军队，雷厉风行，直至取得重大的胜利。此诗描写周王部队很有场景感，以鸟形容其迅速轻捷，以江汉形容其人多势众，以大山形容其稳健，以川流形容其不可战胜，可谓意气风发，神采飞扬。

天何以刺？何神不富？舍尔介狄，维予胥忌。不吊不祥，威仪不类。人之云亡，

邦国殄瘁！

天之降罔，维其优矣^①。人之云亡，心之忧矣。天之降罔，维其几矣^②。人之云亡，

心之悲矣！

觱沸槛泉，维其深矣。心之忧矣，宁自今矣？不自我先，不自我后。藐藐昊天，

无不可巩。无忝皇祖，式救尔后。

荡之什·瞻卬

瞻卬昊天，则不我惠？孔填不宁，降此大厉。邦靡有定，士民其瘵。蟊贼蟊疾，靡有夷届。罪罟不收，靡有夷瘳！

女覆说之。

人有土田，女反有之。人有民人，女覆夺之。此宜无罪，女反收之。彼宜有罪，

哲夫成城，哲妇倾城。懿厥哲妇，为枭为鸱。妇有长舌，维厉之阶！乱匪降自天，

生自妇人。匪教匪诲，时维妇寺。

鞫人忮忒，谮始竟背。岂曰不极，伊胡为慝？如贾三倍，君子是识。妇无公事，

休其蚕织。

Complaint against King You

I look up to the sky;
Great Heaven is not kind.
Restless for long am I;
Down fall disasters blind.
Unsettled is the state;
We're distressed high and low.
Insects raise havoc great,
Where's the end to our woe?
The net of crime spreads wide.
Alas! Where can we hide!

People had fields and lands,
But you take them away.
People had their farm hands;
On them your hands you lay.
This man has done no wrong;
You say guilty is he.
That man's guilty for long;
You say from guilt he's free.

A wise man builds a city wall;
A fair woman brings its downfall.
Alas! Such a woman young
Is no better than an owl;
Such a woman with a long tongue
Will turn everything foul.
Disaster comes not from the sky
But from a woman fair.
You can't teach nor rely
On woman and eunuch for e'er.

They slander, cheat and bluff,
Tell lies before and behind.
Is it not bad enough?
How can you love a woman unkind?
They are like men of trade
For whom wise men won't care.
Wise women are not made
For state but household affair.

Why does Heaven's blame to you go?
Why won't gods bless your state?
You neglect your great foe
And regard me with hate.
For omens you don't care;
Good men are not employed.
You've no dignified air;
The state will be destroyed.

Heaven extends its sway
Over our weal and woe.
Good men have gone away;
My heart feels sorrow grow.
Heaven extends its sway
O'er good and evil deeds.
Good men have gone away;
My heart feels sad and bleeds.

The bubbling waters show
How deep the spring's below.
Alas! The evil sway

Begins not from today.
Why came it not before
Or after I'm no more?
O boundless Heaven bright,
Nothing is beyond your might.
Bring to our fathers no disgrace
But save our future race!

仰望苍天，为何不肯善待我？

如此长久地不得安宁，你降下这等大祸害。

国家不能安宁，百姓如患重病。

害人虫和各种毛病，它们的步履无止境。

罪网不收，如何痊愈？

人家有土地，你就要夺取。

人家有劳动力，你要抢来归自己。

本来应该判无罪，你反倒收进监狱。

本来应该判有罪，你却任其逃脱。

厉害的男人打天下，厉害的女人毁江山。

多美啊这厉害女人，又像猫头鹰又像鸮。

女人有长舌，是祸患的阶梯。

祸乱不是从天而降，生自妇人。

都不用教诲，只要靠近妇人近侍就够了。

害人莫过于诬陷，前后矛盾的谗言。

难道还没到极致？还有谁会这样作恶？

就像商人利润三倍，君子最知道。

妇人不要因为掺和公事，放弃养蚕与纺织。

老天为何惩罚我，哪个神仙不肯赐福于我？

放弃你真正的敌人，那强大的夷狄，反而对我如此忌恨。

你不悲悯没有善意，礼仪更是不伦不类。

人们纷纷逃亡，国家尽是苦难。

苍天降下大网，多么宽广。

人们尽皆逃亡，我心多么忧伤。

老天降下大网，离我们越来越近。

人们尽皆逃亡，我的心多么悲伤。

泉水泛滥奔涌，是因为它够深。

我心中的忧患啊，难道是从今天开始的？

难道不是从我出生之前？难道不是在我出生之后？

苍天冷漠高远，无处不可控制。

不要羞辱你的祖先，请拯救你的后嗣。

　　此诗痛斥了周幽王荒淫无道、祸国殃民的
罪恶，抒发了诗人忧国悯时的情怀和嫉恶如仇
的愤慨。值得注意的是，这首诗同样不能突破
其历史局限性，将罪过放在女性身上。这种思
维方式大概多少可以减轻痛苦：无道之君只要
别遇到红颜祸水，这个世界就能安好。

①优：宽、厚、广。②几：近。

荡之什·召旻

旻天疾威，天笃降丧。瘨我饥馑，民卒流亡。我居圉卒荒。①

天降罪罟，蟊贼内讧。昏椓靡共，溃溃回遹，实靖夷我邦。

皋皋訿訿，曾不知其玷。兢兢业业，孔填不宁，我位孔贬。

如彼岁旱，草不溃茂，如彼栖苴。我相此邦，无不溃止。②

维昔之富不如时，维今之疚不如兹。彼疏斯粺，胡不自替？职兄斯引。③

池之竭矣，不云自频。泉之竭矣，不云自中。溥斯害矣，职兄斯弘，不灾我躬。④

昔先王受命，有如召公，日辟国百里，今也日蹙国百里。於乎哀哉！维今之人，

不尚有旧！

King You's Times

Formidable Heaven on high
Sends down big famine and disorder.
Fugitives wander far and nigh;
Disaster spreads as far as the border.

Heaven sends down its net of crime;
Officials fall in civil strife.
Calamitous is the hard time;
The state can't lead a peaceful life.

Deceit and slander here and there,
Wrong-doers win the royal grace.
Restless, cautious and full of care,
We are afraid to lose our place.

As in a year of drought
There can be no lush grass,
No withered leaves can sprout.
This state will perish, alas!

We had no greater wealth
In bygone years;

We're not in better health
Than our former compeers.
They were like paddy fine;
We're like coarse rice.
Why not give up your wine
But indulge in your vice!

A pool will become dry
When no rain falls from the skies;
A spring will become dry
When no water from below rise.
The evil you have done will spread.
Won't it fall on my head?

In the days of Duke Shao
Our land ever increased.
Alas! Alas! But now
Each day our land decreased.
Men of today, behold!
Don't you know anything of old?

苍天暴虐，降下这沉重的丧乱。

饥馑令我生病，百姓尽皆流亡。

我居住之处都是灾荒。

天降罪网，蟊贼内讧。

昏丧之人无法与共，乱糟糟尽出邪僻事，实在要夷平我邦。

喊喊促促之人，不知道自己的毛病。

兢兢业业之人，反倒不得安宁，我的位置越来越低。

就像当年大旱，野草难以丰茂，就像那水草上岸成枯槁。

我看这个国家，没有哪里不溃烂。

曾几何时，我的富裕今难比，我今日沉疴不过如此。

那糙米与这精米一看即知，小人为何不自退？

坏形势在拉长。

池塘枯竭，从水边开始。

泉水枯竭，从中间开始。

这个灾害很普遍，坏形势在蔓延，大灾到了我自身。

昔先王受命，有像召公这样的臣子，

每日开辟国土百里，如今每天丧失国土百里。

呜呼哀哉，如今之人，没有旧人那样的才干。

　　《诗序》说这首诗是凡伯刺幽王大坏也。但从诗中内容来看，更像是普通人抱怨年成越来越坏，今非昔比。这首诗中值得注意的句子是"皋皋訿訿，曾不知其玷。兢兢业业，孔填不宁"。意思是说，毛病多的人，不会自省，反倒能跟自己的毛病相安无事；兢兢业业之人，想操劳得多，反而日夜不得安宁。此诗结构错落复杂，情感郁愤深沉。

①圉：本义表示关押犯人的牢房，也指边陲边疆。②溃茂：溃即茂。③职兄斯引：兄，通"况"。引，拉长。④弘：扩大。

第五章

旨酒 × 思柔

CHAPTER FIVE

To see if mild is wine

清庙之什·昊天有成命

昊天有成命，二后受之。成王不敢康，夙夜基命宥密①。

於缉熙！单厥心，肆其靖之。②

King Cheng's Hymn

By great Heaven's decrees
Two kings with power were blessed,
King Cheng dare not live at ease
But day and night does his best
To rule the State in peace
And pacify east and west.

苍天有成命，文王武王接受。

成王也不敢偷安，白天黑夜勉力以承天命。

啊，多么光明。

他用尽心力，于是天下安宁。

《诗序》说此诗祭祀天地，朱熹认为是
祭祀周成王之诗。此诗叙述了周初三王对周
王朝作出的贡献，重点赞扬了周成王为完成
先王事业所作的努力。

①基命宥密：基，通"其"；宥，通"有"；密，勉力。②肆：于是。

清庙之什·我将

我将我享，维羊维牛，维天其右之。仪式刑

文王之典，日靖四方。伊嘏文王，既右飨之。

我其夙夜，畏天之威，于时保之。

King Wu's Sacrificial Hymn

I offer sacrifice

Of ram and bull so nice.

May Heaven bless my state!

I observe King Wen's statutes great;

 I'll pacify the land.

O King Wen grand!

Come down and eat, I pray.

Do I not night and day

Revere Almighty Heaven?

May your favor to me be given!

五

旨酒思柔

我奉我献，这些牛羊，老天保佑。

效法文王之典，日日谋求安定四方。

伟哉文王，保佑我，请冥受这祭品。

我白天黑夜忙碌，敬畏老天之威，于是保住这国邦。

《诗序》：《我将》，祀文王于明堂也。祭祀的对象是文王，自称敬老天之威，白天黑夜不敢懈怠，有慎独之意。此诗语言质朴，充满了敬畏之情。

清庙之什 · 时迈

时迈其邦，昊天其子之，实右①

序有周。薄言震之，莫不震叠。

怀柔百神，及河乔岳，允王维后。

明昭有周，式序在位。载戢干戈②，

载櫜弓矢。我求懿德，肆于时夏，

允王保之。

King Wu's Progress

A progress through the state is done.
O Heaven, bless your son!
O bless the Zhou House up and down!
Our victory is so great
That it shakes state on state.
We revere gods for ever
Of mountain and of river.
Our king is worthy of the crown.

Zhou's House is bright and full of grace:
Each lord is in his proper place,
With spears and shields stored up in rows,
And in their cases arrows and bows.
The king will do his best
To rule the kingdom east and west.
O may our king be blessed!

武王巡视诸邦,他是老天的亲儿子,护佑我周国。

当初他出兵,谁人不震惊。

祭祀安抚众神,又至河川高山,我王不愧为世间君主。

周国何其辉煌,诸侯各安其职。

干戈止息,刀枪入库。

追求美好的品德,施行于华夏,周王保佑我们的国邦。

《诗序》:《时迈》,巡守告祭柴望也。
柴望者,两种祭礼,柴是祭天,望是祭山川。
这首诗讲述周王巡游并祭祀天地山川,他主
张文治,以此巩固帝王之业,反映了周人神
化先祖、天人合一的理念。

①右序:右,序,都是"助"的意思。②后:君主。

清庙之什·执竞

执竞武王，无竞维烈。不显成康，上帝是皇。

自彼成康，奄有四方，斤斤其明。

钟鼓喤喤，磬莞将将，降福穰穰。降福简简，

咸仪反反。既醉既饱，福禄来反。

Kings Cheng and Kang

King Wu was full of might;
He built a career bright.
God gives Cheng and Kang charge
This glory to enlarge.
Kings Cheng and Kang are blessed
To rule from east to west.
How splendid is their reign!

Hear drums' and bells' refrain.
Hear stones and flutes resound.
With blessings we are crowned.
Blessings come to our side;
Our lords look dignified.
We are drunk and well fed;
Blessings come on our head.

自强唯有武王，谁比他功业更强。

他将成王与康王之德发扬光大，上天让他成为君王。

他的精神来自成康，使得他终于拥有四方，他目光如炬眼神明亮。

钟鼓响喤喤，磬莞奏将将，老天降福何其多。

祭礼谨慎又庄严。

还望上天醉且饱，让福禄一再降此邦。

《诗序》：《执竞》，祀武王也。这首诗的争议主要在于"成康"，到底是指成王和康王，还是指武王成就康定天下？这里取朱熹的说法。虽然说这首诗是祭祀武王，但是成康二位皆是一脉相承，提及他们也很合理。此诗的重要特色是对乐器齐奏的场景进行了生动的描述。"喤喤""将将""穰穰""简简""反反"等叠字词的使用，使整个祭祀仪式庄严肃穆，让人有身临其境的感觉。

清庙之什·思文

思文后稷，克配彼天。立我烝民，莫匪尔极。贻我来年，[①]

帝命率育，无此疆尔界，陈常于时夏。

Hymn to the Lord of Corn

O Lord of Corn so bright,
You're at God's left or right.
You gave people grain-food;
None could do us more good.
God makes us live and eat;
You told us to plant wheat,
Not to define our border
But to live in good order.

思及后稷之德，可以匹配上天。

养育我等百姓，无人不受你的恩赏。

留给我们麦种，天命以此养育。

不设任何疆界，推广农政于此华夏。

　　此诗是祭祀周族祖先后稷以配天的乐歌。
对于农神后稷的歌颂，怎么样都不过分。这
首诗构设了天人沟通、天人感应的艺术境界。

①来牟：来，小麦。牟，大麦。

臣工之什·雍

有来雍雍，至止肃肃。相维辟公，天子穆穆。

於荐广牡，相予肆祀。假哉皇考！绥予孝子。

宣哲维人，文武维后。燕及皇天，克昌厥后。

绥我眉寿，介以繁祉，既右烈考，亦右文母。

King Wu's Prayer to King Wen

We come in harmony;
We stop in gravity,
The princes at the side
Of the king dignified.
"I present this bull nice
And set forth sacrifice
To royal father great.
Bless your filial son and his state!

"You're a sage we adore,
A king in peace and war.
O give prosperity
To Heaven and posterity
"Bless me with a life long,
With a state rich and strong!
I pray to father I revere
And to my mother dear. "

诸侯来的时候很和睦，到这里很恭敬。

诸侯助祭，天子仪态雍容。

啊，献上大的牲畜，帮助我把祭品铺陈。

伟大的父皇，请保佑你的儿子。

臣子聪明，君王能文能武。

天下和乐，后世子孙能昌盛。

请赐予我昌寿，佐以多福。

请皇考享受祭品，以及我的母亲。

　　武王祭文王，告诉他世间诸事，请求他
享受祭品，赐予自己福寿。一个祭典，既有
丰盛的祭品，又囊括当时的政治要人，可见
其极为隆重。

臣工之什·载见

载见辟王，曰求厥章。龙旂阳阳，和铃央央。

鞗革有鸧，休有烈光。率见昭考，以孝以享。

以介眉寿，永言保之。思皇多祜，烈文辟公。

绥以多福，俾缉熙于纯嘏。①②

King Cheng's Sacrifice to King Wu

The lords appear before the king
To learn the rules he ordains.
The dragon flags are bright
And the carriage bells ring.
Glitter the golden reins,
His splendor at its height.
The filial king leads the throng

Before his father's shrine.
He prays to be granted life long
And to maintain his rights divine.
May Heaven bless his state!
The princes brave and bright
Be given favors great
That they may serve at left and right.

初见周王，求其典章。

龙旗飘扬，横木与旗子上的铃铛响当当。

辔头金饰，美丽有光芒。

率领诸侯祭先王，献上祭礼请品尝。

以求长寿，永远保佑，君王多福。

有功德的各位诸侯，赐予你们诸多幸福，使这大福放光明。

　　此诗是诸侯朝见周成王并助祭于武王庙时，在祭祀仪式现场所咏唱的乐歌，表现出后代子孙对祖先的崇拜与感激之情。此诗铺叙生动，场面隆重，气氛热烈。

①缉熙：光明。②纯嘏：大福。

臣工之什·有客

有客有客，亦白其马。①有萋有且，

敦琢其旅。有客宿宿，有客信信。

言授之絷，以絷其马。薄言追之，

左右绥之。既有②淫威，降福孔夷。

Guests at The Sacrifice

Our guests alight
From horses white.
Their train is long,
A noble throng.
Stay here one night;
Fasten their horses tight.
Stay here three nights or four;
Let no horse leave the door!
Escort guests on their way;
Say left and right, "Good day! "
Say "Good day" left and right
Till day turns into night.

我有嘉客，白马驾车。

随从如云，举止优雅。

他住了一晚又一晚，他一共住了四天。

递根绳子给他，拴住他旳马。

我追随他的脚步，左右之人尽力挽留。

有这样的好品德，大大旳福气馨给他。

　　此诗描写的是宋国微子朝觐周王，离别时国王设宴践行的场面。此诗以轻松欢快的笔调，叙述主客相逢别离的故事，质朴无华，自然流畅，情真意切，洋溢着浓郁的生活气息。

①有萋有且：形容随从很多。②淫威：淫，盛，大。

臣工之什·武

於皇武王！无竞维烈。允文文王，克开厥后。

嗣武受之，胜殷遏刘①，耆定尔功。

Hymn to King Wu Great and Bright

O King Wu great and bright,
Matchless in main and might.
King Wen beyond compare
Opened the way for his heir.
King Wu after his sire
Quelled Yin's tyrannic fire.
His fame grows higher and higher.

　　伟大的武王，您的功业无人能敌。

　　文王的文德，能够为后世开辟基业。

　　武王受之，战胜殷商，阻止杀戮①，奠定您不朽
的功业。

　　这是歌颂周武王克商取得胜利的乐歌。
赞美周武王的文治武功，并且强调他从周文
王那里继承了优秀的德行。此诗气势恢宏，
确为颂诗中的上品。

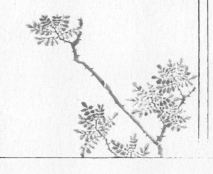

①刘：杀戮。

振鹭
×
于飞

第六章

CHAPTER SIX

Rows of egrets in flight

闵予小子之什·丝衣

丝衣其紑，载弁俅俅。自堂徂基，自羊徂牛，

鼐鼎及鼒，兕觥其觩。旨酒思柔。不吴不敖①，

胡考之休。

Supplementary Sacrifice

In silken robes clean and bright,
In temple caps for the rite,
The officers come from the hall
To inspect tripods large and small,
To see the sheep and oxen down and up
And rhino horns used as cup,
To see if mild is wine,
If there is noise before the shrine
In sacrifice to lords divine.

你的丝绸祭服皎洁，你头戴爵弁端正。

从庙堂走到门边，献了羊又献牛，有大鼎又有小鼎。

兽角酒杯弯弯，美酒味道柔和。

不喧哗也不傲慢，祝大家长寿且美好。

　　此诗是记述周贵族祭毕巡视饮宴安排情况的作品。这是一个非常专业的助祭者，衣着洁净，冠冕端正，循序而来，温和平静。

①吴：喧哗。

闵予小子之什·酌

於铄王师，遵养时晦。

时纯熙矣，是用大介①②。

我龙受之，蹻蹻王之造③。

载用有嗣，实维尔公允师④。

The Martial King

The royal army brave and bright
Was led by King Wu in dark days
To overthrow Shang and bring back light
And establish the Zhou House's sway.
Favored by Heaven, I
Succeed the Martial King.
I'll follow him as nigh
As summer follows spring.

啊，辉煌的王师，韬光养晦。

待到光明之日，方才大动干戈。

我受上天恩宠，威武乃是王之造就。

因此代代传承，效法武三的法则。

　　此诗是周王在秋收后用新谷祭祀宗庙
时所唱的乐歌。祭祀是一年劳作的总结，
这首诗回顾了这一年从春耕到秋收的全过
程，是对祖宗的汇报，也是对自己这一年
的肯定与鼓励。此诗有助于研究西周社会
形态，了解农业生产力的发展，具有重要
的史料价值。

①熙：光明。②介：甲，兵戎。③龙：荣宠。④师：法则。

闵予小子之什·桓

绥万邦，娄丰年。天命匪解，桓桓武王。保

有厥士，于以四方，克定厥家。於昭于天，

皇以间之。

Hymn to King Wu

All the states pacified,
Heaven favors Zhou far and wide,
Rich harvest from year to year.
How mighty did King Wu appear
With his warriors and cavaliers
Guarding his four frontiers
And securing his state!
Favored by Heaven great,
Zhou replaced Shang by fate.

六 振鹭于飞

安定万邦，年年丰收。

应天命而不懈，威武的武王。

保佑这些勇士，用于安定四方。

能够让百姓安宁。

啊，光明现于天空，老天让他君天下而取代商。

　　此诗旨在歌颂周武王的功德无限，其光
彩明著于天，于是上天命令武王替代殷而治
理天下。此诗内容集中，结构紧密，语言流畅。

闵予小子之什·赉

文王既勤止，我应受之。敷时绎思[①]，我徂维求定。时周之命，於绎思。

King Wu's Hymn to King Wen

King Wen's career is done;
I will follow him as son,
Thinking of him without cease.
We have conquered Shang to seek peace.
O our royal decree
Should be done in high glee.

文王勤奋至极，我应该传承他的精神。

发布文王之德，让其绵延不绝，我去征伐，以求天下安宁。

周的运数，哎不要中断。

此诗是周武王在告庙仪式上对所封诸侯的训诫之辞。周武王在赞叹文王之功德的同时，要求诸臣发扬文王勤于政事的精神。该诗语气诚恳，表现了武王深远的忧虑，警示诸侯不可荒淫懈怠。

①绎：寻绎。

闵予小子之什·般

於皇时周！陟其高山，①隋山乔岳，允犹翕河。

敷天之下，②裒时之对。③时周之命。

pÓu

tuÒ

The King's Progress

O great is the Zhou State!
I climb up mountains high.
To see hills undulate
And two rivers flow by.
Gods are worshipped, I see,
Under the boundless sky,
All by royal decree.

哎，伟大的周王！

登上那高山，狭而长的山，高高耸立的山，沈沈之水汇入大河。

普天之下，聚在这里答谢。

接受周的命令。

《诗序》：《般》，王巡守而祀四岳河海也。此诗是写周王巡狩并祭祀山川的颂诗。在巡狩、祭祀的同时，召告诸侯接受命令。

①隋：山之狭而长者。②裒：聚集。③时：承，接受。

明明鲁侯，克明其德。既作泮宫，淮夷攸服。矫矫虎臣，在泮献馘_{guó}。淑问如皋

陶，在泮献囚。

济济多士，克广德心。桓桓于征，狄彼东南。烝烝皇皇，不吴不扬。不告于讻，

在泮献功。

角弓其觩，束矢其搜。戎车孔博，徒御无斁。既克淮夷，孔淑不逆。式固尔犹，

淮夷卒获。

翩彼飞鸮，集于泮林。食我桑黮，怀我好音。憬彼淮夷，来献其琛。元龟象齿，

大赂南金。

骃之什·泮水

思乐泮水，薄采其芹。鲁侯戾止，言观其旂。其旂茷茷，鸾声哕哕。无小无大，从公于迈。

思乐泮水，薄采其藻。鲁侯戾止，其马蹻蹻。其马蹻蹻，其音昭昭。载色载笑，匪怒伊教。

思乐泮水，薄采其茆。鲁侯戾止，在泮饮酒。既饮旨酒，永锡难老。顺彼长道，屈此群丑。

穆穆鲁侯，敬明其德。敬慎威仪，维民之则。允文允武，昭假烈祖。靡有不孝，自求伊祜。

The Poolside Hall

Pleasant is the pool half-round
Where plants of cress abound.
The Marquis of Lu comes nigh;
His dragon banners fly,
His flags wave on the wing
And his carriage bells ring.
Officers old and young
Follow him all along.

Pleasant is the pool half-round
Where water-weeds abound.
The Marquis of Lu comes near;
His horses grand appear.
His horses appear strong;
His carriage bells ring long.
With smiles and with looks bland,
He will instruct and command.

Pleasant is the pool half-round
Where mallow plants abound.
The Marquis pays a call.
And drinks wine in the hall.
After wine, it is foretold,
"You will never grow old.
If along the way you go,
You will overcome the foe. "

The Marquis' virtue high
Is well-known far and nigh.
His manner dignified,
He is ever people's guide.

He is bright as well as brave,
Worthy son of ancestors grave.
He is full of filial love
And seeks blessings from above.

The Marquis of Lu bright
Sheds his virtuous light.
He has built the poolside hall;
Huai tribes pay him homage all.
His tiger-like compeers
Presents the foe's left ears.
His judges wisdom show;
They bring the captive foe.

His officers aligned
With their forces combined
Drove in martial array
Southeastern tribes away.
They came on backward way
Without noise or display.
At poolside hall they show
What they have done with the foe.

They notch their arrows long
On bows with bone made strong.
Their chariots show no fears,
With tireless charioteers.
The tribes of Huai they quell
Dare no longer rebel.
As the Marquis would have it,
The tribes of Huai Submit.

The owls flying at ease
Settle on poolside trees.
They eat our mulberries
And sing sweet melodies.
The chief of Huai tribes brings
All rare and precious things:
Ivory tusks, tortoise old,
Southern metals and gold.

乐哉泮水，可采水芹。

鲁侯到此，看他的龙旗。

龙旗飘扬，鸾铃声哕哕。

无论尊卑，跟随公前进。

乐哉泮水，可采水藻。

鲁侯到此，他的马健壮。

他的马健壮，他的声音洪亮。

谈笑风生，没有怒色循循善诱。

乐哉泮水，可采莼菜。

鲁侯到此，在泮宫饮酒。

饮的是好酒，他以此赐手下难老。

顺着那长路，拿下叛臣做俘虏。

庄重的鲁侯，恭谨地将德行体现于行动。

礼仪恭谨谨慎，是百姓的标杆。

他能文能武，英明有如他祖先。

事事仿效先辈，只求其福。

勤勤恳恳的鲁侯，他的教化能修明。

建好的泮宫，淮夷人民都归顺。

英勇的战士如犯虎，泮宫里献上敌人的左耳。

审问俘虏，精细得像皋陶。

泮宫里献上俘虏，谁也没得逃。

贤士众多，能够发扬德心。

威武出征，涤荡东南。

人山人海，不喧哗，不张扬，不争功，互相诉讼，在泮宫里献功。

弯曲的角弓，一串箭嗖嗖射出。

兵车排成长龙，步兵骑兵不疲劳。

征服淮夷，顺从不再叛逆。

坚定遵照你的谋划，淮夷终于被征服。

猫头鹰翩翩飞，聚集于泮林。

吃我的桑葚，报答我以悦耳之音。

悔悟的淮夷，献上珍宝。

有大龟和象牙，还有大块的美玉和黄金。

这是歌颂鲁僖公平定淮夷之武功的长篇叙事诗。细述鲁僖公征服淮夷之过程，虽然史家考证他其实是被淮夷俘虏。历史上的帝王为祖上贴金是常规操作，若实在无金可贴，就虚构出祖宗的超强能力。

六辔耳耳。春秋匪解，享祀不忒。皇皇后帝！皇祖后稷！享以骍牺，是飨是宜。

降福既多，周公皇祖，亦其福女。

秋而载尝，夏而楅衡，白牡骍刚。牺尊将将，毛炰胾羹。笾豆大房，④ 万舞洋

洋。孝孙有庆。俾尔炽而昌，俾尔寿而臧。保彼东方，鲁邦是尝。不亏不崩，

不震不腾。三寿作朋，如冈如陵。

公车千乘，朱英绿縢。二矛重弓。公徒三万，贝胄朱綅。烝徒增增，戎狄是膺，

荆舒是惩，则莫我敢承！俾尔昌而炽，俾尔寿而富。黄发台背，寿胥与试。

俾尔昌而大，俾尔耆而艾。万有千岁，眉寿无有害。

泰山岩岩，鲁邦所詹。奄有龟蒙，遂荒大东。⑤ 至于海邦，淮夷来同。莫不率从，

駧之什·閟宫

閟宫有侐，实实枚枚。赫赫姜嫄，其德不回。①上帝是依，无灾无害。弥月不迟，

是生后稷。降之百福。黍稷重穋，稙稚菽麦。奄有下国，俾民稼穑。有稷有黍，

有稻有秬。奄有下土，缵禹之绪。

后稷之孙，实维大王。居岐之阳，实始翦商。至于文武，缵大王之绪，致天之届，

于牧之野。无贰无虞，②上帝临女。③敦商之旅，克咸厥功。王曰叔父，建尔元子，

俾侯于鲁。大启尔宇，为周室辅。

乃命鲁公，俾侯于东。锡之山川，土田附庸。周公之孙，庄公之子。龙旂承祀，

鲁侯之功。

保有凫绎，遂荒徐宅。至于海邦，淮夷蛮貊。及彼南夷，莫不率从，莫敢不诺，

鲁侯是若。

天锡公纯嘏，眉寿保鲁。居常与许，复周公之宇。鲁侯燕喜，令妻寿母。宜

大夫庶士，邦国是有。既多受祉，黄发儿齿。

徂徕之松，新甫之柏。是断是度，是寻是尺。松桷有舄，路寝孔硕，新庙奕奕。

奚斯所作，孔曼且硕，万民是若。

Hymn to Marquis of Lu

Solemn the temples stand,
Well-built, well-furnished, grand.
There we find Jiang Yuuan's shrine:
Her virtue was divine.
On God she did depend
And safely by the end
Of her ten months was born
Hou Ji, our Lord of Grain or Corn.
Blessed by Heaven, he knew
When sowing time was due
For wheat and millet early or late.
Invested with a state,
He taught people to sow
The millet and to grow
The sorghum and the rice.
All over the country nice
He followed Yu of xia's advice.

The grandson of Hou Ji
King Tai came to install
Himself south of Mount Qi,
Nearer to Shang capital.
Then came Kings Wen and Wu;
They both followed King Tai.
King Wu beat Shang in Mu,
Decreed by Heaven high.
"You should have nor fear nor doubt
For great God is with you.
You'll wipe Shang forces out,
With victory in view. "

King Cheng said to his uncle great,
"I will set up your eldest son
As Marquis of Lu State
And enlarge the land you have won
To protect the Zhou State. "

The Duke of Lu was made
Marquis in the east obeyed,
And given land to cultivate,
Hills, rivers and attached state.
He was Duke of Zhou's grandson
And Duke Zhuang's eldest son.
With dragon banners at command,
He came six reins in hand.
He made his offering
In autumn as in spring
To God in Heaven great
And Hou Ji of Zhou State.
He offered victims nice
For the great sacrifice
And received blessings twice
From his ancestors dear;
Even the Duke of Zhou did appear.

In summer came the rite;
In autumn horns were capped of bull.
There were bulls red and white,
Bull-figured goblets full,
Roast pig, soup and minced meat,
And dishes of bamboo and wood,

And dancers all-complete.
Blessed be ye grandsons good!
May you live in prosperity
And protect the eastern land!
May you have longevity
And may the land of Lu long stand!
Unwaning moon, unsunken sun,
Nor flood nor earthquake far and nigh.
In long life you are second to none,
And firm as mountain high.

A thousand war chariots were seen;
Each had two spears with tassels red
And two bows bound by bands green.
Thirty thousand men the duke led
In shell-adorned helmets were dressed.
They marched in numbers great
To quell the tribes of north and west
And punish southern state.
None of them could stand your attack.
May you enjoy prosperity!
With hoary hair and wrinkled back,
May you enjoy longevity!
Age will give you advice.
May you live great and prosperous.
To a thousand years old or twice!
May you live long and vigorous
As eyebrows long unharmed by vice!

Lofty is Mountain Tai.
Looked up to from Lu State.

Mounts Gui and Meng stand nigh
And eastward undulate
As far as eastern sea.
Huai tribes make no ado
But go down on their knee
Before the Marquis Lu.

We have Mounts Fu and Yi
And till at Xu the ground.
Which extends to the sea
Where barbarians are found.
No southern tribe dare disobey
The Marquis of Lu's command;
None but would homage pay
To the Marquis of Lu grand.

Heaven gives Marquis blessings great
And a long life to rule over Lu.
He shall restore Duke of Zhou's State
And dwell at Chang and Xu.
The Marquis feasted his ministers
With his fair wife and mother old
And other officers
For the state he shall hold.
He shall be blessed with golden hairs
And juvenile teeth like his heir's.

The hillside cypress and pine
Are cut down from the root;
Some as long as eight feet or nine,
Others as short as one foot.

They are used to build temples new
With inner chambers large and long.
Behold! The temples stand in view.
It is Xi Si who makes this song
Which reads so pleasant to the ear
That people will greet him with cheer.

深闭的庙宇多么清静，城墙坚固，绘饰细密。

赫赫先祖姜嫄，品德纯粹无邪。

依赖上天，无灾无害。

怀胎正好十月，生下后稷，各种福禄降于他。

他知道黍子谷子谁先熟，知道大豆小麦如何种。

待他拥有天下，使百姓学会稼穑。

播下的稷和黍，播下稻和秬。

待他拥有天下，就把禹的功业继承。

后稷子孙无尽，古公亶父是太王。

带民众定居岐山之南，便开始准备消灭殷商。

到了文王武王时代，继续太王的功业。

武王替天行道，征伐殷商在牧野。

他号令兵士"不要有二心也不要有欺骗，上帝时刻监察你。制服殷商大军，能够成为了不起的功绩。"

成王对周公说:

"叔父,将你的长子,封侯于鲁国,开辟你的疆土,
为周室辅佐。"

于是颁令于鲁公,封侯在都城之东。

赐他以山川,还有周边属城。

鲁僖公是周公之孙,庄公之子。

他主持祭祀龙旗飘飘,六根缰绳轻轻摇。

春秋祭祀不懈怠,祭品丰富无差错。

"煌煌上帝,皇祖后稷,请享受这牺牲赤牛,请安
然享受各种祭品,多多地降福给我们。周公皇祖,也赐
福给鲁僖公你。"

秋天举行尝祭,夏天在牛栏里养牛。

白赤色公牛做祭品,牛角杯触碰响将将。

烤猪肉与肉片汤,盛在大的器皿里。

万舞姿态汪洋,孝孙享受吉祥。

"使你的国家繁荣昌盛,使你长寿又健康。保佑那
东方,鲁邦永恒常在。永不崩亏,永不震荡。寿比南山,
如高岭如山冈。"

鲁公战车千乘,矛头飘红缨,弓套缠丝绳,战车插
双矛,人人带两弓。

鲁公步兵三万,头盔镶贝红线连,步兵一层又一层。

击败戎狄,惩罚荆舒,兵势谁敢挡?

"使你国家繁荣昌盛,使你长寿而富有,生出黄发
鲐鱼背,高寿而才干不减当年。让你家国昌盛,让你高

寿至耇艾，千秋万代，高寿而无痛无灾。"

泰山岩岩，为鲁邦人所仰望。

您的权力覆盖龟蒙两地，拥有的疆域到极东。

到那海邦，淮夷诸族也来归附。

没有谁敢不服从，这都是鲁侯之功。

鲁国拥有凫山和绎山，徐宅也是我土。

边境线抵达海邦，淮夷蛮貊，以彼南夷。

没有谁敢不服从，没有谁敢不应诺。

鲁侯之令天下顺从。

上天赐鲁侯以大福，让他长寿，保护鲁国。

常地和许地都在他辖下，恢复当年周公之疆域。

鲁侯安乐，有贤妻和高寿的母亲。

善待大夫与诸士，让国家安宁和平。

他因此多受福祉，生出黄发与儿齿。

徂徕山上的松树，新甫山的柏树，砍之切之做原材，测量其长短。

巨大的松木椽，宏伟的正殿。

这新庙多么美好。

奚斯写下这首诗，才气纵横篇幅长，顺应万民心声。

　　鲁僖公做新庙，奚斯为之写下这首长诗。
此诗回顾鲁国的历史，强调鲁僖公征伐的功
绩，颂扬鲁僖公的文治武功，表达诗人希望
鲁国恢复其在周初时尊长地位的强烈愿望。
此诗为君主唱赞歌，内容上虽不是多取，但
在艺术表现上，却是诗人精心结撰的力作。

①回：邪僻。②虞：欺骗。③敦：治理。④大房：古代祭祀所用的礼器，用以盛牛羊
等牲畜。⑤荒：有。

武王载旆，有虔秉钺。如火烈烈，则莫我敢曷。苞有三蘖，莫遂莫达。九有有截，

韦顾既伐，昆吾夏桀。

昔在中叶，有震且业。允也天子，降予卿士。实维阿衡，实左右商王。

商颂·长发

濬哲维商，长发其祥。洪水芒芒，禹敷下土方。外大国是疆，幅陨既长。有娀方将，

帝立子生商。

玄王桓拨，受小国是达，受大国是达。率履不越，遂视既发。相土烈烈，海外有截。

帝命不违，至于汤齐。汤降不迟，圣敬日跻。昭假迟迟，上帝是祇，帝命式于九围。

受小球大球，为下国缀旒^①。何天之休。不竞不絿，不刚不柔。敷政优优，百禄是遒。

受小共大共，为下国骏厖^②（máng）。何天之龙^③，敷奏其勇。不震不动，不戁（nǎn）不竦，百禄是总。

The Rise of Shang

The sire of Shang was wise;
Good omens had appeared for long.
Seeing the deluge rise,
He helped Yu stem the current strong,
Extend the state's frontier
And domain far and wide.
He was son born from Swallow queer
And Princess of Rong, its bride.

He held successful sway
Over states large and small.
He followed his proper way.
To inspect all and instruct all.
Xiang Tu, his martial grandson,
Ruled over land and sea he had won.

Heaven's favor divine
Lasted down to the Martial King.
Toward his lords benign,
In praise of God he'd often sing.
His virtue grows day by day;
It is God he reveres.
God orders him to hold sway
And be model to the nine spheres.

He received ensigns large and small
From subordinate princes far and nigh.
He received blessings from gods all
For which he did not seek nor vie.

To lords he was nor hard nor soft;
His royal rule was gentle oft.
He received favors from aloft.

He received tributes large and small
From princes subordinate.
He received favors from gods all;
He showed his valor great.
Unshaken, he was fortified,
Unscared, unterrified.
All blessings came to his side.

His banners flying higher,
His battle-ax in his fist,
The Martial King came like fire.
Whom no foe could resist.
Xie Jie was like the roots
Which could no longer grow
When he lost his three shoots,
Wei, Gu, kun Wu, Tang's former foe.
The Martial King destroyed the brutes
And he ruled high and low.

In times when ruled King Tang,
There was prosperity for Shang.
Heaven favored his son
With Premier A Heng to run
The government and state
At left and right of the prince great.

商朝代代有睿智之王，长久地兴发吉祥。

洪水茫茫，大禹造福四方。

将外面大国圈入疆域，幅员多么长。

有娀氏兴起，帝立其女所生之子契，一手建商。

契是威武之王，拿下小国顺利，拿下大国畅达。

遵循礼法不逾越，遍巡四方令能行。

孙子相士也威武，四海同心齐归一。

上帝之命无人违，代代传承到成汤。

汤王出生正当时，圣明谦恭向上。

他祈祷祭祀久不息，真心敬畏上帝，上帝下令，以
他为九州典范。

受大小圭玉，为诸侯表率。

受天之庇护，不逞强不焦虑，不刚硬也不软弱，施
政温和，百禄聚于他。

受大法小法，为天下庇护。

受天之宠，施展其勇。

不震惊也不窜动，不怯懦也不竦动，百禄在他这里
汇总。

　　大旗插在契的车头，坚固的斧钺在手，像火烈烈燃烧，谁能将我遏制？

　　树上若有三枝，就没法长大。

　　九州必须整齐，先扫除韦顾，再涤荡昆吾夏桀。

　　当年在中叶，威严建功业。

　　天子诚信，就有卿士为他而生。

　　就像那位阿衡，他将商王辅佐。

　　这是一首记述殷商发迹史特别是歌颂商汤功德的长篇颂诗。《诗序》：《长发》，大禘也。大禘指的是古代君王祭天地，但这首诗将商汤先祖契的丰功伟绩一并回顾。此诗章句相对，变化多姿，内容凝练，语言匀称，有较强的节奏感，开中国诗词对仗之先河。

①何：通"荷"，承受。②骏厖：庇护。③龙：宠。

商颂·殷武

挞彼殷武，奋伐荆楚。罙入其阻，^①袌荆之旅。有截其所，汤孙之绪。

维女荆楚，居国南乡。昔有成汤，自彼氐羌，莫敢不来享，莫敢不来王。曰商是常。

天命多辟，设都于禹之绩。岁事来辟，勿予祸适，稼穑匪解。

天命降监，下民有严。不僭不滥，不敢怠遑。命于下国，封建厥福。

天命降监，四方之极。赫赫厥声，濯濯厥灵。寿考且宁，以保我后生。

商邑翼翼，四方之极。赫赫厥声，濯濯厥灵。寿考且宁，以保我后生。

陟彼景山，松柏九九。是断是迁，方斫是虔。^②松桷有梴，旅楹有闲，寝成孔安。

Hymn to King Wu Ding

How rapid did Yin troops appear!
They attacked Chu State without fear.
They penetrated into its rear
And brought back many a captive'sear.
Wu Ding Conquered Chu land.
What an achievement grand!

The king gave Chu command,
"South of our state you stand.
In the time of King Tang
Even the tribes of Jiang
Dared not but come to pay
Homage under his sway.
Such was the rule of Shang. "

Heaven gave lords its orders
To build their capitals within Yu's borders,
To pay homage each year,
To do their duties, not to fear
 Its punishment severe

If farmwork is well done far and near.
Heaven ordered the lords to know

The reverent people below.
They should do no wrong nor be
Indolent and carefree,
To each subordinate state
May be brought blessings great!

The capital was full of order,
A model for states on the border.
The king had great renown.
And brilliance up and down.
He enjoyed longevity.
May he bless his posterity!

We climbed the mountain high
Where pine and cypress pierced the sky.
We felled them to the ground
And hewed them square and round.
We built with beams of pine
And pillars large and fine
The temple for Wu Ding's shrine.

殷军疾如闪电，奋勇征伐荆楚。

深入险要之地，俘获荆楚之旅。

所到之处皆归心，汤孙功绩无与伦比。

你们荆楚，居于南方。

昔有成汤威武，纵是氐羌，也不敢不来朝拜，
不敢不来尊我主为王。

说愿意对商臣服。

天命各路诸侯，在大禹治水之地建都。

岁岁来朝，不予惩罚，稼穑不要懈怠。

老天派下巡查官，下民需要恭谨。

不妄为不过分，不敢懈怠偷懒。

命令下方诸国，享受封疆大福。

商邑整齐，是四方之极。

声名赫赫，神灵光明。

长寿又安宁，保佑我的子孙后代。

登上景山，松柏挺拔。

锯而搬之，砍削成可用之材。

松树橡子长长，一行行柱子粗壮，寝庙修成就
此安宁。

　　此诗是祭祀殷高宗的乐歌。其主题是称颂他的武功，讲述他寝庙建成的过程，并祈求国泰民安，福寿惠及王室子孙后代。

①衰：虏获。②虔：梭的假借字，削。

图书在版编目（CIP）数据

呦呦鹿鸣：美得窒息的诗经：汉英对照/许渊冲译；
闫红解析. —— 武汉：长江文艺出版社，2024.2
ISBN 978-7-5702-3296-3

Ⅰ.①呦… Ⅱ.①许…②闫… Ⅲ.①《诗经》–诗集–
汉、英 Ⅳ.①I247.5

中国国家版本馆CIP数据核字(2023)第138860号

呦呦鹿鸣：美得窒息的诗经：汉英对照
YOUYOULUMING；MEI DE ZHIXI DE SHIJING；HANYING DUIZHAO

责任编辑：栾　喜　　　　　　　　责任校对：韩　雨
封面设计：棱角视觉　　　　　　　责任印制：张　涛

出版：长江出版传媒｜长江文艺出版社
地址：武汉市雄楚大街 268 号　　　　　邮编：430070
发行：长江文艺出版社
　　　北京时代华语国际传媒股份有限公司　　（电话：010-83670231）
http：//www.cjlap.com
印刷：三河市宏图印务有限公司

开本：787毫米×1092毫米　1/32　　印张：10.25
版次：2024年2月第1版　　　　2024年2月第1次印刷
字数：130千字

定价：49.80 元